William Butler

MAN IN A NET

Peter Owen · London

ISBN 0 7206 0301 3

BR/BR

PETER OWEN LIMITED
12 Kendrick Mews Kendrick Place London SW7

First British Commonwealth Edition 1971
© William Butler 1971
All Rights reserved

Printed in Great Britain by
Bristol Typesetting Co Ltd.
Barton Manor St Philips Bristol

ONE

Someone switched on a lamp.

Amsden frowned at the edge of the sleep into which he had fallen along the sofa—then blinked; then, abruptly, he opened his eyes widely to find himself being scrutinized by the large Negro who had brought him to this room. The Negro stood at the end of the sofa, before the lamp table, his hand still on the lamp switch. The fixity of his huge brown eyes gave Amsden a queer sensation of being neuter —he might have been an unexciting poker hand that the Negro was determining how to play.

'You fell asleep, charley,' the Negro said quietly, dropping his hand slowly. 'That's pretty good—falling asleep.'

Amsden slowly brought himself up into a sitting position, placing his hands on the seat of the sofa and moving his legs forward, as if he meant to rise to his feet; but he only sat there. In a moment he glanced at his watch, murmuring :

'Eight-twenty . . . I did fall asleep.' Glancing up, his voice was more taut : 'Look, aren't you about ready to tell me why you brought me here?'

'Boss'll do that,' said the Negro with an expressionless civility. He turned to stroll to the only door of the room. 'Sorry I had to wake you, Professor, only company's coming. Thought I'd see how you were making out.' He snapped on the ceiling lamps.

'Company?'

'You betcha,' said the Negro. He opened the door, peered out into what was apparently a dim corridor. He must have seen nothing, for he only closed the door again and leaned back against it. 'Yeah,' he said. 'Company. Another suspect, charley.'

'Suspect,' mused Amsden—and suddenly yawned. He shook his head and rubbed his lined forehead with aggravated fingers, then squinted at the Negro. 'When are you going to understand that you captured the wrong body? Nothing else makes sense.'

The Negro's huge eyes gazed back at Amsden emptily.

'My friend,' said Amsden, presently sighing and leaning back in the sofa, giving his head one small shake, 'I'm aware it doesn't serve much to keep saying it, but I'll try once again : if you're hoping to improve your social status this fiscal year at my expense, you're going to be so much wiser and just as poor in the morning. Say—look, I'll tell you what : I know Nelson Rockefeller's address. Will that help? But there is no one, no one in this world, who'd pay ten cents for *me*. Dead or alive. No one. Nowhere. Tell you the truth, I wouldn't pay it myself.'

'Even the college wouldn't pay for you?' asked the Negro with a bored solemnity. He seemed only vaguely curious. 'Don't they value you?'

'My friend, Lit. teachers are two cents a pound this year,' smirked Amsden. 'And institutions of higher learning don't pay ransom money. You have to stay on your toes just to keep them paying salaries.'

'That right, charley?' mumured the Negro, unimpressed.

Amsden kept glowering upon him. 'Nelson's address doesn't grab you?'

The Negro puckered his mouth and slowly shook his head—then all at once turned and opened the door, having heard something in the corridor.

A man considerably shorter than himself, yet nearly as

hefty—the barrelish breadth of his chest and roundness of his shoulders contrasted with the slenderness of his waist and hips to give him the look of a girdle-wearer—marched quickly into the room, scowling beneath his head of thin red hair. He seemed at first to be moving alone, but at the last moment he was pushed from behind and stumbled his way into the room, then swung about to scowl at the small, wiry Chinese behind him, crying, 'Don't do that! I got a bad heart!'

'Hey, you got bad heart?' asked the bright-eyed Chinese, mouth gaping with real or mock surprise.

'I already told you I do!'

'But me same!' grinned the Chinese, nodding and touching his chest. 'Me got vely bad heart—sure! Him same,' he gestured at the Negro who had opened the door. 'Him got number one collupt heart. Sometime I say myself, all men got bad heart: got to give push to get ahead in world. So I push.' The Chinese turned to grin at the Negro. 'Bang bang!' he said, pointing a finger.

Now the redhead swung round to face Amsden, who had sat forward in the sofa again. The redhead positioned himself before Amsden, legs apart and feet solidly on the rug, fists clenched at his sides, seeming to bolster himself against a physical attack.

'O.K. Mister,' he nodded at Amsden, his voice shaking with rage, 'you tell me! What's it all about? No one ever tried to shove me around before, and I'm mad. Plain *mad*! I'm so mad I'm worried for my blood pressure and my heart. So you get down to business right now, and whatever the problem is, let's solve it. Because I'm telling you for your own good, you better let me walk back out that door within five minutes. Five minutes—you understand? Now: what in hell am I doing here?'

Amsden glanced at the Negro at the door—who wore only the tracery of a smile—then looked back at the angry newcomer. He said, 'I'm willing to bet you're a suspect.'

'I'm a what?'

'A suspect.' Seeing he made no impression on the red-head, Amsden shrugged a shoulder.

The redhead stood sputtering. He apparently could not make his brain ingest the idea or get his mouth around the word for a minute, then cried : 'A suspect!' He looked back at the Chinese, at the Negro, glared heavily at Amsden. 'A suspect of what? Listen, who are you? I don't even know you!'

'I'm Harry Amsden,' said Amsden, crossing his arms on his chest, exploring the redhead's face with thin, unamused eyes. 'I was hoping I'd know *you*.'

The redhead shook his head, still glaring. 'No—I never saw you before. And I'm not glad to meet you. Listen, are you going to get down to business or not? What's this farce all about, goddam it?'

'I wouldn't know,' said Amsden. 'I'm only a suspect, like you.'

The redhead's scowl somehow managed to grow deeper. He seemed to regard Amsden's reply as a clever evasion.

'Ask them,' Amsden suggested, nodding off towards the Negro and the Chinese.

The redhead blinked around, his scowl quivering.

'Bang bang!' grinned the Chinese, pointing a finger at him.

'What's this all about?' the redhead asked the Negro.

'Man, you're all worked up so sassy,' said the Negro softly. 'There ain't nothing to get het up about.'

'Goddam it, you clear it up right now!' The redhead took a step towards the Negro and planted himself solidly again. 'I'm not a well man. My heart can't take this sort of thing, at my age.'

'How old are you, charley?' asked the Negro.

The redhead scowled briefly before answering. 'Fifty-two.'

'Hey, man,' the Chinese grinned slyly, cocking his head. 'You're putting us on.'

'Shut up!' snapped the redhead. He looked at the Negro.

'What's the matter with him? All the way here, he plays the dumb Chinaman and other pronunciation games. He's crazy.'

'Poverissimo pubertissimo!' cried the Chinese. 'I'ma try to be simple China boy, I'ma know my place, and you calla me k'rayzee. What I gotta do—be black, likea my friend? Atsa aska too much, I no be black!'

The Negro nearly managed a wry grin before asking Amsden soberly, 'How old are you, Professor?'

'Forty-six,' said Amsden.

The Negro nodded, then said, 'Man, you look older.'

'I think too much,' muttered Amsden.

'You don't want to do that,' said the Negro, gathering the Chinaman in the embrace of one arm, turning him to the door. 'Say, you two charleys make yourselves at home. We'll have our last delivery pretty soon, and the boss'll come and answer all your questions. Hey—anything sensible you charleys want? Smokes? Drinks?'

'Coffee,' suggested Amsden.

'That's like cooking man,' the Negro shook his head. 'We ain't cooks. Smokes or a drink I could offer you.'

'Water, then,' mumbled Amsden.

'You betcha.' The Negro freed the Chinese. 'Charley's thirsty, buddy.'

'I hully quick,' grinned the Chinese, opening the door. 'I no let cholly-boy suffer.' He winked at the redhead. 'Bang bang!' he said, then quickly stepped out and shut the door after him.

The Negro leaned against the door again, stuffing his hands in his pockets. 'Carson City'll be right back.' He looked at the redhead. 'Whyncha sit down?'

'What did you call your friend?' squinted Amsden.

'My buddy?' asked the Negro. 'That's Carson City Go, Professor. Fastest gun in Jersey. He's a good boy.'

'He's a goddam double-talking Chinaman gangster!' exclaimed the redhead in a rage. 'That's what he is.'

The Negro pondered and nodded thoughtfully. 'Sure,

9

charley,' he said. 'He's kind of damned, kind of Chinese, and a first-rate gangster. But don't say any more, man. That's my buddy.'

The redhead rubbed his teeth together and looked down, then stuffed his hands in his pockets. 'How long are you going to keep me here?'

'Gee, I don't know,' said the Negro tonelessly. 'Whyncha ask the boss when he gets here?'

'All right,' nodded the redhead. 'Who's the boss?'

'Whyncha ask the boss when he gets here?' returned the Negro, lowering his head and suddenly taking a few steps towards the redhead. 'You're all het up and sassy. You ought to sit down, charley—take it easy.'

'Take it easy,' growled the redhead, backing away from the oncoming Negro. 'How can I—'

The Negro set a hand softly on the redhead's shoulder, which silenced him, and the black hand led the redhead to the sofa, turned him, prodded him to sit. The redhead sat.

'There you go, charley,' said the Negro placidly. 'Ain't that better?'

The redhead scowled as deeply as he could and again his hands were clenched into fists. He glanced from beneath this scowl over at Amsden, at the other end of the sofa.

'Can I ask a question?' Amsden inquired of the Negro.

The Negro, strolling back to the door, said, 'You betcha.'

'What was that about another delivery?'

The Negro, turning to lean against the door again, only gazed at Amsden.

Amsden frowned and presently drew a leg up, holding his hands about the knee. 'You said I could ask a question.'

'You did,' said the Negro.

Amsden nodded and sighed, then looked bleakly at the redhead. Looking back at the Negro, he said, 'Another suspect, I presume.'

The Negro smirked at the redhead. 'Man, you better cool it. You're scarlet. You look like a chillipepper. Cool it.'

This advice started the redhead trembling, as if the very thought that he should not be furious in this situation was enough to redouble his anger. He hit his knee with a fist, leaned forward, again his mouth had difficulty forming words. He sat back and looked helplessly at Amsden. 'I'm so goddam mad,' he squeaked. 'I'm so goddam *mad*!'

Amsden blinked and muttered, 'Don't let it throw you. Maybe it's all going to turn out to be some kind of over-sized practical joke.'

'Joke!' cried the redhead. 'That Chinaman brought me here with a gun.' He shook his head violently. 'That was no joke.'

'Carson City Go,' mused Amsden. He moved his eyes to the Negro again. 'And what's *your* name?'

The Negro kept gazing at him.

'Excuse me for my interrogative,' said Amsden, sighing.

Momentarily the Negro said, 'They call me Everybody.'

The redhead snorted, 'Everybody calls you *what*?'

'Lancelot Everybody,' said the Negro. The two captives only looked at him, so he added, 'That's the name you got to live with tonight, anyhow.'

Amsden ran a hand through his sandy hair and sat back. 'Lancelot Everybody and Carson City Go, and I'm apprehended as a suspect. Wow. This is going to be quite a night.' He faced the redhead again. 'I didn't get your name?'

'Koster,' mumbled the redhead, frowning and averting his eyes. 'Cassius Koster.'

Amsden nodded, then said. 'Cassius Koster of Koster and Jones? The publisher?'

'That's right,' the redhead put his frown on Amsden. 'Who are you, again?'

'Harry Amsden. I teach Lit. at Kingston . . . maybe you saw my *Turbulent Mainstream*?'

'What's it?' asked Koster. 'A book?'

Amsden's brows flicked up and down and he looked at his knees. 'Yes.'

'All *I* want to know,' Koster's eyes flashed back to the Negro at the door, 'is why I'm here and when I can go. Why won't you tell me?'

'You cool it,' said the Negro.

'You realize what you're doing?' demanded Koster.

The Negro put his hands back in his pockets. 'What am I doing, charley?'

'The penalties for kidnapping are severe,' said Koster, 'even if you pick up a nobody. Well, I'm no nobody—you understand?'

'What's a nobody?' asked Lancelot Everybody.

'You understand me,' Koster charged angrily. 'You understand me perfectly well. I've got my own friends. Connections.'

The door opened, making the redhead start, the Negro standing aside as the Chinese came in with a tray. On the tray was a large pitcher of water, two glasses and a plate of cream biscuits.

'I bling cookie,' grinned the Chinese, setting the tray on the short table near the sofa, then folding his hands before his stomach and bowing to Koster. 'Confucius say : suspect with happy tummy is happy suspect. Hello ! I make you happy?'

'Shut up,' barked Koster.

The Chinese put his hands on his hips and observed the redhead gloomily for several seconds before turning to the Negro. 'Let's play poker, Lanny.'

The Negro opened the door.

'Listen !' cried Koster, all at once, as the two were about to depart. 'Wait—'

The Negro and Chinese looked back.

'I have to urinate,' said Koster.

'An important man like you?' asked the Negro. He gave Carson City Go's sleek black hair a quick rubbing with one hand and said, 'You want to take him to the bathroom, buddy?'

'All my life I want that!' cried Carson City Go with overdramatized ecstasy. 'Gleat opportunity now mine—I see if white devil sit or stand. Come 'long, white devil!'

Koster's scowl had chilled on the Chinese and he muttered, 'Never mind.'

'You don't go with Go to go?' asked the Chinese.

Koster said, 'I'll wait.'

'Man, it may be a long wait,' said Lancelot Everybody.

Koster still scowled, but his scowl wavered with indecision. He patted his knees nervously and finally rose, trudging across the room to join the Chinese, who let him walk on ahead into the corridor.

The Negro shut the door and leaned against it again. He and Amsden stared at one another for a while before the Negro said, 'That's a weird charley my buddy brung you. Tough luck.'

'Oh, it could have been worse,' said Amsden, stretching his arms up. He shook his head sharply, then rose to his feet. 'I'm sure I'd rather chat with Mr Koster than *you*, for example.' He had taken out his cigarettes, stuck one in his mouth and now felt about his pocket for matches. He started to glance around the room, as if thinking he had left his matches here or there. 'I don't suppose you smoke.'

'No,' said Everybody. 'But I got matches.'

'Much obliged,' said Amsden, meandering over to the Negro, still fishing about in his pockets. 'I seem to have dropped mine.' The Negro's hand had just withdrawn a book of matches from his coat pocket when Amsden, in front of him, all at once hurled a knee towards the Negro's stomach and shot an arm out to grab about his neck. The Negro, so easily it seemed a gesture of tolerance, caught the threatening arm, turned it and had Amsden not gone spinning instantly backwards, the twisted arm must have broken. He spun all the way to the sofa, falling on it.

Slowly, he got himself back into a sitting position. Lancelot Everybody threw him the book of matches.

'Thanks,' murmured Amsden.

'Keep 'em,' said the Negro.

'Thanks,' nodded Amsden, and his hands shook as he lit a match and lifted it, only to find his cigarette was no longer in his mouth. It lay on the floor near Everybody, who bent to pick it up and tossed it to Amsden.

'Thanks again,' Amsden said. He lit another match and managed to get the cigarette alight from the unsteady flame.

The door opened and Carson City Go shoved Cassius Koster into the room, as roughly as before.

The Chinese giggled. 'Him speak tluth, got vely bad heart. Him tly obstluct poor China boy doing duty—assault me! No warning! Two fist on my poor head!' He held his head, shook it between his two hands as if the pain was still there. 'I much surplise, I say: oh please no hurt China boy. Him not heed. So I lough him up little bit. Him plenty O.K. now'

During this performance, Koster had stumbled to the sofa and sat, breathing heavily; and suddenly he emitted something like a sob. He covered his lowered face with a large hand, and did not uncover it until—hearing the door shut and the lock snap—he looked between his fingers to see that Lancelot Everybody and Carson City Go had left the room. Gradually, he released his fingers from their grasp on his face and brought his hands down into his lap.

Koster sat shaking his head to himself for some while, then for some while longer only stared glumly at the rug. Amsden had smoked down a new cigarette before Koster mumbled, 'That little bastard pistol-whipped me.' He glanced shortly at Amsden. 'You read about such things. . . .' Then he covered his face again, and another soblike sound spurted out from between his fingers. 'My poor wife, my little honey-girl, oh my God.' He dragged his hands down. 'I wonder how much they're asking.'

'How much are you worth?' asked Amsden, beside him.

'Not a hell of a lot,' said Koster. He looked over. 'You?'

'My bank account stands at about three hundred dollars, give or take a bum check. I kept trying to tell Sir Lancelot he had the wrong man.'

Koster shook his head and looked down into his open hands. 'You read about things like this,' he said once more and sighed. 'You think they're going to harm us?'

'Since I don't know why I'm here,' said Amsden, 'I can't make a guess what their intentions are. Or even who they are. I kept thinking about it, but got tired.' He nodded towards the door. 'Old Sir Lancelot, he told me I'm a suspect. You too.'

'It's ridiculous,' grunted Koster. 'They're being cute.'

'Maybe.'

'What do you mean, maybe? It's ridiculous. It's money they want. It's that simple : money.'

'They won't get any from abducting me,' remarked Amsden. He fell thoughtful, fingering the knot of his tie, then shook his head. 'I don't know. I was thinking maybe someone's out for vengeance. Maybe someone figures I hurt him.'

'Who?'

'I haven't the vaguest,' Amsden admitted, and stood up. He walked across the room to the door and touched the knob, slowly and silently turning it. He looked back at Koster. 'It's locked all right.'

Koster kept his eyes fastened on Amsden. 'You mean like someone sent me a book I couldn't publish, and maybe he has it in for me? Christ—we turn down twenty goddam manuscripts every goddam day. Everyone in the United States wants me to publish some lousy book. It could be anyone.'

Amsden asked, 'What did you try with the Chinaman?'

'Aw hell,' muttered Koster, knotting his hands to fists

and staring at them. 'I thought maybe I could throw my weight on him. That little guy, he's stronger than he looks. And he had that pistol.' He looked up. 'I got it right across the face. Does it show?'

Amsden wandered over to peer down into Koster's face. He shook his head. 'Little rash is all. He probably didn't hit you as hard as you thought.'

'He hit me plenty hard!' Koster retorted, rubbing his cheek.

Amsden stood back. 'We had the same idea. I had a go with the big black panther while you were out. He treated me like a tennis ball—bounced me across the room.'

Koster was not listening. He was again holding his cheeks, his face lowered, and he began to moan. 'What's happened to me, what's happened to me?'

Amsden stepped over to pour himself a glass of water. 'Well,' he said, 'I don't guess it's your simple every day kidnapping. Water?'

'No. What did they do to you?'

'Do to me?' Amsden lifted the glass, glancing over.

'How did they get you?'

'Oh.' Amsden sipped and slipped his free hand into his jacket pocket. 'I was easy. Sir Lancelot did it all by himself. There I was, wending my cheerful anarchic way home, just off campus, and there was a car there. Sir Lancelot had a map spread out over the steering wheel and his lap, and called me over to ask if I could help him locate a street. I leaned into the car and found out he had a gun under the map. He asked me to sit down and shut the car door.' Amsden smiled, sipped again. 'I did. He made sure he had the right gent, then, and no sooner learned I was *the* Professor Harry Amsden of Kingston College than I was on my way. Don't know how I merited the attention—but here I am.'

'Well, why'd you *do* it?' demanded Koster angrily. 'Why'd you get in the car? Why didn't you call for help?'

Amsden chuckled. '*A,* he was big. *B,* he had a gun. *C,* being myself a kind of social anarchist I first of all thought he was F.B.I.—I'm still not convinced he isn't; but anyhow, I'm a pacifistic anarchist. And *D,* I never felt my pacifism so urgently as when I saw that big gun.'

'You weren't such a pacifist when you jumped him a few minutes ago,' Koster reminded him accusingly, sounding as upset with Amsden as though by his consent to his own abduction Amsden had somehow participated in Koster's abduction as well.

'He didn't have his gun out,' explained Amsden. 'Even so I lacked confidence. You know, when I was twelve I used to have this thing about golden gloves—I wanted to be a champ. Then when I was thirteen I went on my first date and made a pass at a girl. She knocked me out. Since then I've tried to depend on my wit; except you can see where that's got me.' He chuckled and carried his glass back to the sofa, sitting down at the end opposite from Koster again. 'Wow, that giant there—I didn't ruffle him. I just asked for a match and—'

'Let me tell you that little Chinaman is no pushover either,' interrupted Koster with a fierce nod. 'That gun slapped my face so hard I went numb. It was like novocaine. I didn't know if I still had my teeth.'

Amsden chuckled again, crossing his legs. 'They aren't very funny, that's a fact,' he said. 'So I asked for a match and went up to him and tried to punch a knee into him. He whirled and twirled me back to the sofa, then gave me some matches and said, "Keep 'em".' Seeing Koster look off worriedly, Amsden merely chuckled to himself, muttered, ' "Keep 'em",' and sipped at his water.

'I mean,' said Koster, 'what would we be suspects *of*?'
Amsden shook his head.

'Say—do you have a press at the college? Could it have something to do with some book we both know about?'

Amsden touched the rim of his glass to his lip, then said, 'The only thing I have to do with publishing is to observe how my own one and single book grows more obscure with every passing week.'

'Who put it out?'

'Stang and Cranbourne.'

'Oh yeah? Who was your editor—Harding?'

'Mr Cranbourne. You know people there well?'

'I never met Cranbourne. I know Stang.'

'Very well?'

Koster shook his head, then leaned forward, elbows on knees, staring at the door. 'You suppose they're out there? In the hall?'

'There's a little room at the end of the hall I noticed,' said Amsden. 'I figure that's where the poker game's happening.'

Koster studied Amsden shortly. 'How long you been here?'

Amsden glanced at his watch. 'Since about four-thirty.'

'And that's all he told you all this time? That you're a suspect?'

'Mr Koster, I had to work hard to get *that* out of him.'

Koster studied his fellow suspect a moment more, then snapped his tongue and suddenly stood up. 'What about the window?'

'In terms of escape?' asked Amsden. 'Have a look for yourself.'

Koster appeared only shakily able to support himself on his legs and stood uneasily for some seconds, brushing his hands down his jacket. Finally he was able to get his legs moving and he crossed uncomfortably to the window.

'Grilled over,' he said.

'Yep.'

'Sure is dark out there.' Koster pressed his nose to the glass.

'Yep.'

'I sure don't like it,' Koster added gloomily.

Amsden chuckled.

'I don't like it,' muttered Koster, turning to wander back to the sofa, head down. 'My poor honey-girl. My poor wife, when they get in touch with my family, my little girl and my wife, they're going to be in a real bad way.'

'Well . . . maybe they won't be getting in touch with them.'

'That's ridiculous,' snorted Koster. 'How would they raise money except by going through my family?'

'Presuming it's money they want.'

'Of course they want money! They aren't doing this free of charge no matter what the gimmick is. And you can damn well bet we're the ones who'll be doing the paying.' He began to glance sharply around the room. 'Did you look around?'

'Look around what?'

'The room.'

'What for?'

Koster marched over to a high cupboard, three drawers beneath and the five shelves above lined with books.

'What do you expect to find?' asked Amsden.

'How would I know what I expect to find when I don't even know what I'm looking for,' mumbled Koster, on his knees. 'Something to tell me who they are, what they want out of me.' He had opened a drawer, shaken his head, shut it; opened the next below it. He fished about its contents with impatient fingers. 'Playing cards. Maybe we should play poker, Damson. Little roulette wheel . . . bunch of games.' He all at once chuckled sardonically.

'What's funny?' wondered Amsden.

'Clue,' answered Koster. 'Game of Clue.'

Amsden smiled up some irony. 'Say, Koster—you suppose this is the study and I'm really Professor Plum and you're Colonel Mustard? Or look, maybe we've been spirited off by someone writing a detective story, just to see how people act in such a situation.'

'With real guns?' snapped Koster, taking Amsden seriously. He looked up with a mocking sneer as Amsden came to stand by him. 'Kidnapping someone with my heart history?'

'Maybe they don't know your heart history.'

'Well they should!' Koster frowned, then went back to fussing about in the games drawer. 'They should. Or if they don't, they should damn well find out the state of a man's health before trying this sort of thing. No matter the goddam reason for it.' He slammed the games drawer shut, pulled open the bottom drawer.

'There's one of your books here,' said Amsden, taking out a single book from a centre shelf of the bookshelves.

Koster looked up. 'Which one?'

'*The Deaths of Others*,' Amsden read the title. 'By Leonard Hanna.'

'Hanna,' scoffed Koster, all at once making his whole face a twisted revulsion. 'That guy's a creep. A guy like that could *do* a thing like this.'

'Who is he?'

'A creep.' Koster shoved the third drawer shut. 'Bunch of linens is all. Anything else of mine there?'

'I'm looking. Here's one published by Stang and Cranbourne. Collection of Chekhov.'

'Christ, that collection was edited by a teacher up at Syracuse. Someone told me even Syracuse University Press turned it down, never mind their own man did the translations. Stang is really hard up for fiction, you know.'

'Maybe I should write fiction.' Amsden's finger followed the spines of books while his eyes quickly read both titles and publishers of all the books on the shelves. 'Here's another one of yours. Language series.'

'Language series?' Koster frowned at him. 'We don't put out language series.'

'*French for Adults*,' said Amsden. 'Published by Koster and Jones.' He pulled the book out.

'Language series,' Koster muttered, shaking his head disgustedly. 'That's no language book, that's a play. And it'd still be running if the local police were a little more shy of acting as censors for the public at large. Don't you follow theatre?'

'Not so much.' Amsden studied the book. 'I remember, yes. Only you see a title like that and your first thought is it's probably a clean little book that contains what it says it contains. Yes, sure—that was the one where after the whole cast stripped down, they tried to get the audience to take their clothes off too. I thought of coming down to see it, but it had rather a short run.'

'It's a good clean piece of dirty fun,' frowned Koster. 'You got to have faith in numbers if you have faith in people, and that play was on fiction best seller lists for two months. So how many off-beat plays ever hit that list? I'll tell you how many,' Koster said, snatching the book and holding it protectively. He glanced at the title page. 'One—that's how many: *French for Adults*. No other play ever did that.'

'I guess the publicity didn't hurt,' said Amsden.

'What in hell's wrong with publicity?' Koster asked irritably. 'People don't pay attention to publicity unless it tells them something they want to be told.'

'Namely, nakedness and all it promises.'

'Say, what kind of literature professor are you anyhow, if you can't recognize the name of the most controversial play of last year when you see it?'

'I have no beard,' muttered Amsden, looking at the books again.

'What kind of book was it *you* wrote?' asked Koster, setting the copy of *French for Adults* carefully back into its place.

'Criticism.'

'You're a critic and you—'

'Novels only,' said Amsden. 'And don't get me wrong: I have nothing against *French for Adults,* or even for children of a certain age, if it comes to that. It's all so much grist for my happiness mill, all this taking off of clothes, and it's rather fun on the side. More power to you, and I hope you have many more such clean dirty bestsellers . . . but you don't seem to have any more of them right here. Those seem to be the only two books published by Koster and Jones that caught the attention of our secret admirer.'

'Admirer,' mumbled Koster, looking around the room again, as if for more drawers to search. He saw none. 'My poor little girl, my poor wife. Poor little honey, she's going to be so scared for her daddy. Are you married Mr Damson?'

'Amsden.'

'Yeah?' Koster looked at him.

'My name,' said Amsden. 'It's not Damson—it's Amsden.'

'Yeah,' murmured Koster, who wandered over to the water. 'Why the hell did you ask for water when I need a drink?'

'Why didn't you ask for one?' Amsden kept examining the books morosely. 'I don't drink.'

'Why not?' Koster asked, taking up a biscuit and chewing at it nervously. 'I thought you were an anarchist.'

'If it will comfort you,' Amsden smiled wrily, 'I try to enjoy the vices I can. I use grass, hash, girls, demonstrations, even recommend a little violence in others when I'm not present. But I don't happen to drink. Has a bad effect on me.'

Koster carried his water slowly to the sofa, not sipping from it, only gazing glumly down into it. He sat and growled, 'A suspect—me! It makes me so goddam mad!'

'Anyhow,' said Amsden, finding no book to interest him beyond those he had named and drawing out the book entitled *The Deaths of Others* once again, turning to face the sofa, 'better keep your emotions in check. You could need your energy tonight.'

Koster watched Amsden amble back to the sofa, paging through the book. 'You married, Professor?' he asked brusquely.

'Nope.' Amsden sat down, examining sentences.

Koster kept watching him. Soon he asked, 'Why not?'

Amsden peered over at the redhead. 'Why should I be?'

Koster shook his head. 'Nothing. I just wondered if it had to do with your anarchy.'

'Well,' said Amsden, examining the book again, 'as a matter of fact I guess it does. Marriage is kind of an old-fashioned piece of rigmarole, Mr Koster. If you like it, enjoy it, but it gives me the creeps.'

'What the hell good is life without marriage?' demanded Koster.

'What good is it *with* marriage?' returned Amsden. 'Possessiveness, jealousy, overadjustment, boredom and, for girls, the promise of slavery. Little girls have brighter futures these days, however. Which, incidentally, means little boys have more fun. Bigger boys, too.'

'You're a nut,' muttered Koster, and looked off.

Amsden shook his head, then went back to his book, paging more deeply into it.

'You're a nut,' muttered Koster. 'You aren't married—you don't have a daughter going to school. You have no stake in life, so what's it matter to you what's right—so long as you have a good time?'

Amsden shut the book, flattened his mouth and frowned challengingly at Koster, but Koster only whispered something to himself and took a swallow of water, refusing to look at Amsden. Amsden trained his frown down on the book, then the frown cleared from his brow. 'Sure,' he said softly, 'I remember Hanna—the modern Messiah, the Essene with ten thousand gods someone called him. He had that experimental community over in Turkey—right?'

'Yeah,' said Koster, rather sneering at the book he had published. 'He still has it. He's a creep.'

'Why did you publish him then?'

'It's a book, isn't it?' scowled Koster. 'I run a business, not a tyranny. I publish things I don't agree with too.'

'Or, in other words, you'd publish a photographic essay

23

of Christ in drag in the valley of the dolls, if you thought it would earn a profit.'

'If I thought it was art I would,' affirmed Koster at once. 'Why not?'

'Why not indeed,' smiled Amsden, who sighed and rose and went to take himself another glass of water. He lifted the glass in a toast to the publisher.

Koster snorted and looked away, and soon fell to sighing broadly, deeply. Amsden strolled vacant-faced about the room and Koster covered his eyes with one hand.

'None of it makes sense,' said Koster. 'It's all like *Alice in Wonderland*.'

'Or Kafka,' suggested Amsden. 'I mean, if we're suspects, presumably there's a judgement day a-coming. Or maybe it *is* Judgement Day.'

'None of it makes sense,' repeated Koster. He suddenly leaned over to snatch a biscuit from the plate on the lamp table, angrily popping it into his mouth. He scowled at Amsden as he devoured it. 'If we're both suspects of the same thing, we must have some connection. What connection do we have?'

'Search me,' said Amsden. 'But I hope we aren't *both* guilty.'

'What do you mean?'

'Well, I mean,' Amsden chuckled, 'it'd be nice to think at least one of us has a chance of going home tonight.'

'What do you mean?' Koster was alarmed. 'You think only one of us is going to be allowed to leave?'

'I only wish I knew,' said Amsden. 'And wish I knew who we have for a mutual enemy.'

Koster shook his head furiously. 'I don't have that kind of enemy. Even my enemies aren't criminals.'

'Well . . . someone thought enough of you to bring you here.' Amsden faced the window again, running a finger along the pane.

'So what in hell are you saying, Professor Damson?'

Amsden glanced over his shoulder. 'Amsden,' he frowned.

'Yeah, yeah—so what are you saying?'

'All I said is, we have an enemy in common.'

'Who?'

Amsden, pacing slowly back towards the door, shook his head. At the door he bent and peered into the keyhole, then said : 'Guess what I see.'

'What?' Koster demanded.

'The back of a key.' He stood up. 'I've seen films where someone pushes the key through the slot after sliding a piece of paper under the door. The key falls on the paper, you pull it through—eureka! Only, I'm not going to do it.'

'I wouldn't.' Koster waved his hand out against the idea. 'They'd hear. That'd be the end of us.'

Amsden was now strolling for the bookshelves, found them uninteresting and wandered over to one of the two high overstuffed wing chairs at angles to the sofa, plopping down into one of them, muttering a curse of impatience under his breath. He ran a finger across one of his eyes, then said, 'Maybe we should try to figure out who our enemy is.'

'Look, it's just going to be some nut,' insisted Koster. 'Someone who has it in his head you're responsible for something and I'm responsible for something, so he's going to get himself some money out of it. He's a nut, that's all.'

'Sure, but if there's going to be a trial in this particular castle, why not try to be a little prepared for the defence? It would be nice to have some answers ready, because whoever it is—well, I don't suppose he's going to appoint us a defence attorney.'

Koster's face trembled into worry and he said more quietly, 'You really think some creep's trying to take out a grievance on us?'

'That's exactly what I wish we could figure out. All I know for certain is, I was euphoric, anarchic and on my way home, when this car stopped and Sir Lancelot, obviously meaning business, thought I should—'

'Where in hell are we anyhow?' Koster interrupted.

'Could you follow the route? You said Jersey? I thought we were still in New York, at least. If they've crossed a state line, I guess they really *do* mean business.'

Amsden sipped water. 'I think we're in Jersey. And it's kind of deserted in these parts—I think the nearest neighbour was about two miles down the road.'

'Yeah,' muttered Koster, who had apparently observed as much for himself. He glared at the rug silently, then sighed and suddenly lifted his glass and drank his water down quickly. He contorted his face to evince some displeasure with the water and set his glass aside. Leaning back into the corner of the sofa, he drew a leg up onto the cushion and proceeded to stare at Amsden glumly. 'Well,' he said after a time, 'what's the dark deed, Professor, that made some goddam lunatic wonder which one of *us* did it?'

They tossed names and places back and forth and came up with nothing. Amsden paced a circle about the large chair he had been sitting in, hands behind his back and head down. Koster's eyes were shut tightly and his thinly drawn lips suggested the wariness he felt towards the explorations they were pursuing.

Amsden said as he paced, 'Let's go back to the beginning. You know Stang and I know Cranbourne.'

'Yeah,' said Koster, opening an eye on Amsden. 'So what?' The second eye opened. 'I wish you'd sit down. Say—you didn't ever offer that book of yours to one of my editors? My editors are nuts.'

'No.' Amsden had stopped, as if in deference to Koster's nervousness, but then began to pace about the other of the two large wing chairs. Koster followed him with an irritated eye. 'And I don't suppose your daughter ever studied at Kingston?'

'Hell no.'

They glanced at each other.

Amsden took another stroll around the chair, then sat

in it and crossed his legs, waggling a foot and staring off at the door. 'We're going at this the wrong way. The question isn't who we know—it's what have we *done*? It's something one or both of us did that's got someone mad enough to want to get back at us.'

'Well, I've done nothing, goddam it!' snapped Koster, squeezing the knee of the leg folded on the cushion. 'I told you : I'm just a business man, plain and simple and straightforward, and that's all I am. Naturally, there are times I come out ahead of someone else, but that's in the game. I get a book someone else wanted. Someone gets a book I wanted. Someone gets my writer, I get someone else's writer.'

'Ah, but *how* do you get someone else's writer, Mr Koster?' Amsden fingered his tie and leered at Koster.

'By taking a financial risk—that's how. It's completely legitimate. Completely. It's not even unusual.'

Again there was a stillness, and they gazed at one another.

'Look, you compete too,' scowled Koster. 'What the hell, *all* life competes. You compete on your level, that's all.'

They kept their shared gaze steady until Amsden said, 'We aren't being honest with each other.'

'What do you mean?' snapped Koster.

'We're reacting like we're prosecuting each other—but pretty soon someone's going to come in here and do some real prosecuting.'

'So? What are you driving at?'

'We just aren't being very revealing with each other, that's all,' said Amsden, beginning to waggle his foot again.

'Why should we be?'

'Because that's about the only way we're going to find out what the hell is happening to us, Mr Koster—that's why.'

Koster thinned his eyes, glancing down at his knee, then shook his head and shifted about, snuffling, running a hand across his face, groaning and finally looking at Amsden to say, 'Yeah, so I tell you the story of my life and it turns out all I say has nothing to do with this. Why should I want to tell you my secrets?'

'To compare secrets, of course,' Amsden shot right back. 'My God, how much time do you think we're going to—'

'What are you after?' Koster interrupted madly. 'Say—ever since I came in this room, you've been pressing me. Now you want the private details of my life. I'm damned if I don't think you're one of *them*. What are you after, anyhow?'

Amsden put his teeth together and pushed a whistling sigh out from behind them, shook his head, stood up. Finding his circle about the chair with absent feet again, he just muttered, 'Nothing. Forget it.' He snatched out a cigarette, lit it. 'Cigarette? You smoke?'

'With *my* heart?'

Amsden passed by the table in his pacing to drop a match into the ashtray there.

'I mean,' Koster began, and nervous excitement rather than anger lifted his voice, 'why start with me? Okay, maybe we got to try and figure it out—but why start with me?' He rubbed the palms of his hands together. 'And I don't suppose *you've* got any real crimes on your conscience, either?'

Amsden grinned sourly, glancing at Koster as he strolled. 'I suppose I've practised my share of mayhem against most of the commandments, Mr Koster. I prefer to call myself an anarchist rather than an immoralist, but I don't pretend I'm not the ego behind my actions—which is what most people seem to do, isn't it? You have to be the good guy, and never admit you were ever anything but the good guy. No . . . you've got your secrets. You didn't get to the top on an elevator, you got there on a staircase made out of human beings.'

'What the hell business of yours is it whether—'

'Because,' Amsden wheeled on him, his voice biting, 'one of those people you stepped on, Mr Koster, may be responsible for what's happening to both of us tonight—me as well as you.'

'I never stepped on anyone!' Koster flashed back as bitingly. 'Get off my back, Professor!'

Amsden went back to his pacing, stopping at the ashtray to flick ashes from his cigarette.

'Teachers, writers, intellectuals,' Koster mumbled to himself, and shrugged a shoulder contemptuously. 'I've known too goddam many like you. You're all a bunch of misfits. And you want to teach everyone else how to run the world.'

Amsden stopped where he found himself, towards the window, to wheel on Koster again. 'You give us a hand, Mr Koster—in the name of a little profit for yourself. You publish us.'

'Yeah!' Koster nearly snarled, squeezing his knees once more. 'Yeah, that's what I do. I publish what I don't agree with as well as what I like. Sometimes for money, sure—but I'm not the only publisher who looks for the real thing. How the hell do you think important stuff *does* get published? Listen: it's tough finding a real writer, and it's pretty goddam sad when you find out someone in your position—a teacher, goddam it—thinks the whole business is unprincipled. Jesus, what does that make you with your teaching novels except some kind of pimp?'

'I get along,' muttered Amsden, resuming his stroll to the window. 'The teacher's job is kind of like a critic's: sucking the meanings out of things.'

'Well, suck away, you sucker,' whispered Koster. He seethed inwardly for a minute, then said in an even voice that still seemed addressed more to himself than at Amsden: 'Now and again, not so often but now and again, you do find a writer. Someone with a message, someone with class. You bring him into the public eye, give him a boost. In a way, you're responsible for him. It gives you a feeling of reward.'

Amsden, as evenly and privately, faced the window as

he muttered, 'I'll bet it does.' He turned and headed for the ashtray.

'Craig Haigman, for example.' Koster followed Amsden with cynical eyes. 'I literally made him.'

'I'll bet you did,' murmured Amsden, pushing his cigarette out in the ashtray.

'The way Max Perkins made Tom Wolfe,' said Koster. 'By writing his goddam book for him. And it sold.'

'I'm sure it did,' said Amsden, sighing as he saw he was heading right back for the window.

'I'm not saying Haigman doesn't have talent,' Koster added quickly. 'If he didn't have talent, I couldn't have helped him.'

'We aren't getting anywhere,' Amsden said, looking out into the darkness. 'Craig Haigman obviously loves you. The question is, who hates you?'

'I wouldn't know. Who hates *you*?'

'Sometimes I think everybody.'

Koster twisted a thumb towards the door, scowling. 'That guy?'

Amsden glanced back, frowning at Koster's thumb, then chuckled. 'Sure,' he said. 'Him too. In fact, I'll tell you something, my friend : the only thing that surprised me utterly in finding myself brought to this particular prison was how little it surprised me at all—how little I was shocked to learn someone holds me suspect and wants me alive or dead.'

Koster shook his head, unable to derive any meaning from the statement. 'Well, why?' he demanded. 'What the hell did you do?'

'Everything—but it isn't just what I did. It's the sense of having *done* things, the sense of being responsible, the miserable sense of having to go on with the destruction because, what the hell, I feel like *I* dropped the bomb on Hiroshima, *I* was old Joe McCarthy, *I* suggested to General Westmoreland he make himself a Christian Crusade in Vietnam, I was—hell, I'm Dallas, I'm George Wallace,

Lester Maddox, J. Edgar Hoover, for Christ's sake. And at least part of the reason I have to exist as all these things is because there are too many people like you who don't give any part of a damn!' Amsden's voice was not loud, but was bitterly cold, accusing, and his mouth sneered before he blinked, relaxed his features, put his hands in his pockets and went back to his pacing. 'Outside of that, my friend, I've contributed my share of earnest anarchist sin to the world. Like I say, I use girls, grass, whatever the old body can tolerate. I taught a course in sex one year. Well,' he chuckled, stopping to face Koster, who stared at him open-mouthed, 'that was before I was sure of my anarchist faith, actually. I wondered what the girls and boys would make out of direct confrontation with a certain kind of literature, if it would make them reflect on the morality they inherited or the morality they wanted the world to have. Wow,' he shook his head, chuckled a bit more, turned and paced again. 'The results were frightening. That's when I gave way to total anarchy. If you can't beat 'em, at least lay 'em.' He was smiling as he faced Koster next. 'You don't look impressed.' Koster's face wore a locked-in bewilderment. 'Well . . . let's see. What else did I do? Well, I borrow money and don't pay it back.'

'That's bad!' exclaimed Koster 'How much did you borrow?'

'Oh, fifty bucks here, a hundred there.'

'And you never paid any back?'

'Sure, you know . . . five here, ten there.'

'That's bad,' Koster shook his head. 'It's a wonder people went on loaning you.'

'I think sometimes, Mr Koster, folks thought it was easier loaning me than not loaning me. I can get pretty upset with a friend who isn't indeed when I'm in need. I resort to nasty names and even occasional blackmail.'

Koster nodded, as if to say he would have expected no better of Amsden, and shut his eyes. He tapped his fingers against his thigh. 'Who'd you borrow the most from?'

Amsden shrugged. 'Fellow named Cal Simon. I owe him a cool four hundred bucks by now.'

Koster squinted at Amsden. 'Four hundred?'

'Approximately.'

'No,' Koster shut his eyes again. 'This sort of thing is no four hundred dollar operation. How much you owe in all?'

'Everyone?'

'Yeah.' Koster was squinting at Amsden again.

'Jesus, I don't know. Borrowers never keep accounts, but . . . well, maybe a few—'

'Maybe,' interrupted Koster, seriously, 'they got together, like a syndicate—all these guys you owe.'

The thought amused Amsden and set him to pacing some more. 'Yes, that's a possibility. Let's see, well, over the years I must be behind a few thousand dollars.'

Koster looked disappointed. 'Only two thousand?'

'Don't look so let down. It's enough to make a teacher a lonely man on campus.'

In a minute, Koster wondered, 'How did you get on with your students?'

'Pretty good. They taught me how to be a professional anarchist.'

'Aw, hell,' muttered Koster, setting his leg down on the floor, dashing a hand back through his thin red hair. 'This is silly.'

They fell into a silence, each meeting the other's glance and, for some reason, each beginning a scowl that made their eyes separate. Koster looked at the floor and when Amsden next looked at him, all the wariness seemed to have left his face in favour of simple weariness.

'So who do you know in New York?' asked Koster.

'Cranbourne.'

'Yeah, yeah—who else?'

'I have a cousin there.'

'You said you aren't married. Romance?'

'Naturally,' said Amsden, sitting on the arm of a wing

chair. 'I'm human. It's an important part of my politics.'

'Current?'

Amsden frowned, pushed his legs out, ran his hands up and down his thighs and said softly, 'We may have come to the moment of truth.'

Koster kept his thin eyes on Amsden, waiting.

'Well, I'm fairly deeply involved,' Amsden finally went on, 'with a pretty little thing of splendid old stock who, adoring me beyond all my deserts, insists she's going to kill herself if I tell her to be gone forever. Which, by the way, I have to date had no interest in telling her, anyhow. She's cute.'

'You mean to marry her?'

'With *my* heart?' Amsden grinned quickly.

'Yeah. . . .' Koster sniffed and averted his eyes.

'I am unalterably opposed to marriage as the basis for any personal or social relationship. Besides that, I'd have a sense of guilt: she's eighteen, I'm forty-six.'

'Student?'

'Student,' nodded Amsden. 'A child. A Lolita—and I am not quite yet a Humbert Humbert.'

Koster all at once sat up erect, glaring at Amsden. 'I nearly had that goddam book!' he declared angrily. 'I had it in the palm of my hand—here! And it got away!' He glared at Amsden so fiercely he seemed to be challenging Amsden to suggest there could be a worse piece of luck to befall a man.

'Tough luck,' muttered Amsden.

'Can you imagine how many nights I haven't slept,' asked Koster with his fierce eyes, 'just thinking about that?'

'I sleep pretty easily,' Amsden murmured.

'Yeah?' Koster sighed and stood up, snatched a cookie from the tray and walked slowly to the window. 'Goddam, I wish something would happen. I'm edgy as hell. Eighteen,' he looked around at Amsden and snorted softly. 'That's *way* too young for you. That's disgusting.'

Amsden, hunched over now on the arm of the wing chair, said nothing.

'You pretentious intellectual bastards,' said Koster. He thrust his hands into his pockets and faced Amsden as if meaning to work off his edginess on him. 'Everyone knows you spend half your time going for the girls. My little honey, she goes to Radcliffe—and even that scares hell out of me. Even that. I really didn't want her to go to college at all.'

'You were wise.'

'Yeah. What do you mean? How can *you* say that? You're a teacher, an anarchist—hell, what do you care?'

'I only meant,' Amsden turned his lowered face a bit towards Koster, 'you were wise to think that way if you're really worried for your conservatism as symbolized by your little girl's chastity. Don't mistake my frankness for concern, Mr Koster. It's just that there's exactly as much sex as education on campus these day, and girls react a great deal differently—a great deal more emotionally to both intellectual and physical freedom than boys do. That's all.'

Koster nodded sharply, as if to suggest he had seen something more in Amsden's remarks than their words indicated. 'Yeah—anyhow,' he said, 'she goes to a girl's school. And as far as freedom's concerned, why the hell *shouldn't* girls be free as boys?'

'Methinks,' Amsden said quietly, not facing Koster, 'I sense contradiction in yon pale mind.'

Koster was scowling again. 'How in hell can an anarchist be an anti-feminist, too?'

'It's possible,' said Amsden. 'But in fact, I'm *not* an anti-feminist. Every Independence Day, I send gift packets of the pill to all the girls I know.'

Koster waved a disgusted hand at Amsden and turned his back on him. 'You're a nut,' he muttered, facing the window. He said it again when, after some moments, he turned to walk to the high cupboard. 'You're a nut.' He knelt before the cupboard and opened the games drawer.

'This girl, this eighteen-year-old—do her parents know about you?' He was nervously shoving things about in the drawer.

'What are you looking for now?' asked Amsden.

'I don't know—something to distract myself. I'm edgy as hell. What's the girl's name?' He brought from the drawer the small roulette wheel and, rising, began to spin it and scowl at it as he watched it whirl.

'Sydney Carol.'

Koster's eyes snapped sharply over to Amsden and stung the teacher with some sort of challenge, though Amsden could not understand what the challenge might be. Koster at length looked at the roulette wheel again, gave it a spin as he wandered to the table with the tray upon it. He grabbed a cookie. 'Carol? Her Christian name?'

'Family name.'

Koster sat down and munched solemnly at the cookie, not facing Amsden. 'I don't suppose . . . any relation of Terry Carol? Terrence P. Carol?'

'That's her father,' said Amsden, 'if he's in pharmaceutics and Providence, respectively.'

'Hell,' muttered Koster, looking down at the roulette wheel in his lap. He gave it a half-hearted spin.

'You know him?'

Koster waited for the spinning wheel to stop, then said, 'I don't know. Maybe we're catching on to something.'

Amsden suddenly looked as gloomy as Koster, and stood to move back to the other end of the sofa. Sitting, he asked, 'How well do you know her father?'

Instead of answering, Koster gave Amsden a sour eye and asked testily, 'What did you do to the girl?'

'*Do* to her?' Amsden peered over. 'What kind of question is that?'

'You know what I mean.'

'*Now* who's getting personal?'

Koster, with an abrupt gesture, loosened his tie, then gave the roulette wheel another spin.

35

'I told you,' Amsden said : 'It's a romance, an affair—not just a string of bull sessions.'

Koster spun the wheel more sharply. 'You son of a bitch.'

'Why? Because I live in my times?'

'You're a teacher!' Koster snapped, scowling over.

'That's right!' Amsden snapped right back. 'A teacher—not a priest.'

'My God,' muttered Koster, shaking his head and looking off towards the cupboard. 'Teachers. I wonder how my little honey is making out at Radcliffe.'

'Oh, she's probably making out fine,' Amsden said softly.

Koster's face reddened instantly and he snarled, 'What in hell's the *matter* with teachers these days! My God, you can't leave your little girl in the same room with a *teacher* any more!'

Amsden sighed, tapped his foot against the rug, locked his hands together and stared down at them. 'We don't get paid much,' he said. 'We have to cut corners—make our own incentives.'

'Goddam cynical bastard,' moaned Koster, suddenly more forlorn than angry. 'My God—you don't know how conservative Terry Carol is. I don't know . . . maybe he *is* capable of this sort of thing.'

Amsden imitated Koster's dejection and after a time mumbled, 'Toss me a cookie.'

Koster reached for one and sighed deeply as he handed it across to Amsden.

'So,' said Amsden, cookie in his mouth, 'what would Carol have against *you*?'

Koster rolled his lips around, his gloomy eyes fast on the roulette wheel. 'Did she—the girl, did she talk much about her family?'

'Not an awful lot,' said Amsden. 'Nothing that helps me account for this.' He was watching the door now, and cocked an ear, as if he had heard something.

Koster, catching his glance, frowned worriedly at the door, then started as Amsden stood up.

'What is it?' asked Koster.

Amsden went to the door and set his ear against it. He turned back vacantly, apparently having decided his ear was at fault. 'Did you have any serious set-to's with her father?'

Koster only became meditative. 'It makes me so goddam mad, all of it.' But there was no madness in his tone or his eyes as he watched Amsden. 'You wild bastards,' he went on, his voice again like a moan, 'you *destroy* people and call it philosophy. Where in hell's your common sense?'

Amsden, still at the door, said, 'It's common sense for a solid professional anarchist to indulge in a little destructiveness now and then—not that I think of a love affair as destructive.'

'You don't, huh?'

'You never indulged?' smiled Amsden, a tightly aloof smile.

'What if she became pregnant?' demanded Koster. 'What if she *is* pregnant? Is she?'

Amsden laughed, paced back to the sofa, picked up the book he had left there and began to walk about the room paging through it. 'If all the boys at Kingston suddenly descended upon all the girls at Kingston, Mr Koster, you might or might not see a little special propagation. The modern college girl's breakfast is orange juice and a pill— and I might add, incidentally, Terrence P. Carol's own pill has come into particular fashion at Kingston since Sydney became a student there.' Since Koster only sat shaking his head disgustedly, Amsden went on in a sardonic tone, 'I gather your own daughter hasn't yet learned the pill exists?'

'Don't you bring my daughter into this,' growled Koster. 'She's never even, I doubt if she's ever, I'm,' he sputtered enragedly, 'I'll bet she's never taken a pill in her life!'

'Not even an aspirin?'

'My God—if I caught my honey-girl living that sort of life. . . .'

Amsden grinned at Koster. 'You modern sires sure do set your own traps. So anxious to convince yourself a girl is a human being with all the rights and privileges on the one hand, and that your particular girl would never take advantage of her rights and privileges on the other—but why not, Mr Koster? What makes you so sure?'

'I know because I'm her father!' Koster retorted quickly. 'You got no real relationships, Damson—so a father-daughter relationship is something you just wouldn't understand.' He blinked and looked away, then mumbled, 'Terry Carol . . . my God, but *this*.' He suddenly leaped up and marched to the window to stare out, and Amsden heard him hissing or mumbling to himself. Eventually he said, 'It's so goddam dark. I can't see a light anywhere. There aren't even any neighbours.' He swung around. 'Look, what if it all comes down to one plain issue : that Terry Carol wants to make sure you and his daughter split up? Are you going to agree to that?'

Amsden frowned and smiled together as he lifted his eyes from his book. 'You make Mr Carol sound like a pretty hopeless lunatic.'

'What do you mean? How? I mean, he's tough, he's too old-fashioned and he doesn't take to people very easily —but I don't think he's a nut.'

'No,' smirked Amsden. 'It's just that he seems to think it's reasonable to abduct me and make me a prisoner till I agree to stop going with his daughter—that's what you'd call sane? And will he kill me if I refuse to stop seeing Sydney?'

The publisher watched the teacher morosely, then lowered his head and faced the window. 'No, that doesn't make sense, either.' He threw his arms out and dropped them, 'The whole goddam thing can't make sense!'

Amsden, in his strolling, was soon standing beside Koster at the window. 'Tell me about her father,' he said quietly.

Koster blinked at the dark glass and only said, 'No, I can't understand it. Terry Carol's eighteen-year-old daughter getting interested in you. I mean, if she's anything like her—'

Koster stopped and both gazed from the window nose-to-glass as they heard the sound of a humming engine outside. The two bent their cheeks against the pane as the sudden bright beams of headlights twisted into a driveway beneath, and a car moved by below them in the darkness, its tail lights disappearing around the corner of the house.

Amsden walked back to the sofa with his book, sat down and flicked its pages with a nervous thumb. Koster kept his cheek to the window but finally turned to look at the door, then at Amsden.

The publisher walked to the table by the sofa and poured himself a fresh glass of water. 'Water?' he asked brusquely.

'Please,' murmured Amsden.

Koster poured a second glass and handed it to Amsden, then sat at his end of the sofa, sipping and keeping his eyes on the door.

'Jesus,' muttered Amsden after a time.

Both stared at the door.

Koster all at once growled, 'I'd give an advance of fifty goddam thousand dollars if someone could write me a book telling me exactly what's gone wrong with these goddam times.'

'You're on,' said Amsden, slightly lifting his glass in a toast to Koster.

'Believe me,' Koster shook his head, 'you aren't the man to write that book. Amsden—you *are* the times.'

'That's right,' Amsden responded lightly. 'So you get a first-hand report. Twenty-five thousand?'

Koster whispered a curse.

They both watched the door.

'What's holding them up?' Koster whispered angrily.

In a moment Amsden suggested, 'Maybe they're cooking the hemlock.' And in a few moments more he yawned and said, 'I should have stayed asleep.'

'Who could sleep here?' demanded Koster.

'I managed to for a few hours.'

'Here? *Here?*'

'Sir Lancelot woke me up. Because you were coming.'

'How could you sleep in a situation like this?'

'I used to think if I could just sleep my life away, maybe I could keep death from taking me by surprise.'

Koster's eyes were thin and only briefly on Amsden's face before returning to the door. 'Damson, you're not normal.'

'I keep disillusioning you. Sorry.' He stood, stretched and said, 'And by the way, when do you start unfolding *your* tangled existence?'

'I don't have secrets like that,' Koster threw his eyes to Amsden as briefly as before. 'I never taught pornography, at least.'

'No, you only publish it, so that lets—'

'What in hell made you do a thing like that anyhow?' Koster interrupted. 'Didn't you think nature had enough power to take care of itself?'

Amsden went to the window, peering out. 'The reason was moralistic enough : I was a simpleton and thought an examination of the mores of our times might reveal some thoughts, maybe even some second thoughts, to my youngsters. I wanted to make them think about feelings instead of just feel them.'

'That's a dumb ass thing to want to think about.'

'Is it?' Amsden kept peering out, then looked up. He shaded his hand against the glass to obstruct the reflection of the room-light and said, 'Star light, star, bright, first star I see tonight, I wish I may, I wish I—oh, oh!'

'What?' Koster started, sitting forward.

'I see *two* stars. Second star cancels my wish. Just when I needed one.' He sighed and turned tiredly about, studying the door dismally. 'Well, I learned more than I taught, and I taught what I learned. As for the course you ask about, they ate it up. They ate every sexy idea and word up, and then ate each other up. They clearly meant to eat *me* up next, so I called the whole thing off. Mr Koster, I was too late : they had already learned to worship sex somewhere, and merely wondered why I was so old-fashioned as to think they didn't know what Lawrence, Burroughs and Company had to teach—I mean, there was literally *nothing* those kids didn't know. I wasn't so arrogant as to think kids had nothing to teach me, and they sort of relished that side of my character, deeming me educable. I had sort of planned to take them on field trips, but they took me instead. Underground films, nude plays—this was before *French for Adults*, Mr Koster, but I can assure you it was better than burlesque. It's funny the way it happened, but I gradually began to see they were right and I was wrong—I was a square standing on the sidelines, pretending to some good old-time socialism but failing to see . . . well, not seeing, for example, what Sartre saw : obeying the moral impulses of the *status quo* is serving the *status quo* as a pillar—which is to say, a little moral disobedience, even if you call it fun, is the medicine that's needed these days. Just fun. Since then I've been avoiding what you called a dumb ass thing.'

'What's that?' snapped Koster.

'Thinking about feelings. I've been feeling more and thinking less, and even my cigarettes taste better that way.' He smiled and lighted a cigarette to emphasize his argument, then finished : 'And that is the story of my sex course.'

'You're a nut,' said Koster. 'All you care about is sex. You're a sex nut.'

'My friend,' said Amsden, passing by the sofa and snatching up the book he had been leafing through, carrying it back to the window, 'I'd rather be a user than what you call a pimp. At least I'm not a mere financial profiteer. Now, your philosophy is transparent enough, Mr Koster : if someone can give you a profit on the penis unadorned, then bring in that penis tomorrow—but leave your little girl alone.'

'Intellectual son of a bitch,' muttered Koster. 'You can take your hedonistic theories and—'

Koster cut himself off and rose to hurry to Amsden's side, at the window, as they heard the sound of an automobile engine and tyres on gravel once again. They watched together as the lights of this car, too, slowly by-passed the window, going around the house in the same direction as the previous car.

'Was that the same car?' asked Koster.

'I don't know. I don't think so.'

They both turned to the door.

'I can't stand it any goddam more,' Koster muttered.

'Yeah,' whispered Amsden, who moved head down back to the sofa, sitting to stare at the book he held. Koster was about to follow him to the sofa when they heard the lock at the door being turned. The publisher froze, his hand moving to his heart as the door opened.

It might have been the rather silly, not far from childish, grin the chubby man wore, or simply the fact that he walked in last, but it seemed clear to both Amsden and Koster at once that the last man in was a colleague of Lancelot Everybody and Carson City Go. Ahead of him, with the Negro and Chinese to either side, there was a fourth man, escorted into the room with a ceremony of courtesy.

'I don't think you got to wait too long, charley,' the Negro was saying in pleasantly modulated tones. 'The boss is already here, he's just going to finish freshening up, then he'll be here.'

The pale, short man addressed by Lancelot Everybody was balding on top, bewildered all over his face, and stumblingly uncertain in his gait. The Negro's hand seemed to be introducing an honoured guest to honoured acquaintances as he waved first to Koster, then to Amsden, introducing them, concluding :

'These charleys are real gentlemen. Mr Amsden teaches literature at Kingston College and Mr Koster, he's a man with connections of his own.'

The third suspect, looking dazedly at Amsden and Koster, shook his head as if to reject the possibility of gaining any intelligence from these introductions, and he glanced once more at the Negro, then at Carson City Go, then at their colleague, the grinner behind him. He started to say something, but the word spurted out in a weak cough and he shut his mouth : getting his mouth back open, he said :

'Well, this won't do,' his words expanded by a deep drawl that doubled most of his vowels. 'No, no—this won't do. I really must be allowed the use of a telephone.'

'Aw,' said the too cheerful, curly-haired and chubby new colleague, 'gosh, sir, but what would *you* do if a guest asked *you* the use of his telephone the minute he had got brought into line, like we say, I mean, before the boat was steady, even?' His gravelly voice seemed to add whispers of ridiculing laughter to his nonsensical sentiments. 'Sorry,' he grinned, 'wrong number.'

'Oh, my,' the Southerner remonstrated weakly, managing only the most uncomfortable chuckle, 'I wish you'd stop talking that way. I really do. All you do is ask questions, but I need answers, here.' He looked at Koster. 'I have very kindly and all too patiently wondered about the purpose of these dramatic if playful proceedings for a good while, now, and perhaps it's time for an answer.' He faced the Negro. 'My schedule for tomorrow is very heavy and . . . .' His voice simply dropped off as he gazed into the Negro's vacant face.

Koster all at once rose, stuffed his hands into his pockets, frowned in considerable consternation and asked the newcomer, 'Say—aren't you Harmon Wade?'

The Southerner turned gratefully, almost greedily, on Koster, smiling, 'Yes, sir—I am! Thank you! And I wonder if you could simply inform me what is being celebrated here. Now, I can't make these rare gentlemen understand at all how a busy man, no matter how much he enjoys a little game sometimes, just hasn't always the time to indulge himself.' Harmon Wade freed a short gasp of modest laughter, turned to the three men by the door— two sober faces and one fixedly unnatural grin—and his attempt at merriment faded. He scratched his neck and blinked at them, then frowned.

The Negro opened the door and his two colleagues stepped out, Lancelot Everybody pausing to say, 'Boss'll be along soon. You get desperate for anything, just pound on the door, charleys. We'll hear.' Then, abruptly, he shut the door.

They heard the lock being turned.

'Thank you,' murmured Harmon Wade, vaguely, more as a matter of form than because he could have expected the vanished Negro or anyone else to observe his decorum. He lifted a hand to the door, held it briefly high, then dropped it, shook his head and looked at Koster, then Amsden, then Koster again. He chuckled, but when the chuckle had died, he looked only worried. 'Well, I kept telling myself I was being corralled for a party for some old Lone Star crony, if not myself. But I surely don't know either of you—do I? You aren't Texans?'

'No, sir,' said Amsden, 'we aren't.'

'No,' said Wade. 'And I don't know you?'

Amsden shook his head. 'But perhaps you might know a certain Terrence P. Carol?'

'Carol?' Wade seemed to taste the name as he fingered his cheek, looked back at the door, again at Amsden. 'Well, I know the name of course—you mean the medicine man?—but I never met . . . .'

'My God,' mumbled Koster, not having moved from

where he had simply stood at the sofa, ogling Harmon Wade. 'They kidnapped a congressman.'

Wade slid his hands into his jacket pockets, took a step towards Koster, smiling uneasily. 'Oh, I can't think I've been kidnapped. Such things happen, but this isn't a banana republic yet and—well, it's all a prank, surely.' He was glancing about the room. 'You were both brought here as I was—by surprise?'

'By surprise,' smirked Amsden. 'I guess that's putting it correctly enough.'

'It's annoying, all right,' Wade looked at Koster, 'and I was tempted to scold myself for always shooing my secret service boy away, and yet—well, even the name of that fellow who brought me here is a joke. "Rexie My Riddle", was all the name he'd give, but he certainly lived up to that one—propounding riddles is his favourite pastime. But he was lighthearted, very much in fine spirits—in fact, as best I could guess from his riddles, it was just *sure* to be a party. He told me I was a suspect, for example; so I asked him what it was I was suspected of, and he asked me how it was a man might think his brightest flame wouldn't arouse a little suspicion. Things like that,' he chuckled. Wade turned and walked to the door to try the knob gently.

'The key isn't a joke,' Amsden said. 'It works.'

Wade turned back and sighed. 'I really am ashamed of myself. If that fellow hadn't caught me at the rump-end of my tea-time cocktails, you know, I would never have been so trusting.' He gaped about the room a bit more. 'I'd hate to think it was a plot of some kind . . . that I let a good mood lead to the embarrassment of the whole,' he shook his head and wandered towards the window.

Amsden muttered to Koster, 'Rexie My Riddle—meshes well enough with Lancelot Everybody and Carson City Go, doesn't it? Koster, I think *I* know who's behind this operation.'

'Who?' asked Koster.

'Ring Lardner.'

Koster said, 'He's dead,' and sat down.

'*Is* he?' asked Congressman Wade from the window, and pulled at the lobe of one ear. 'I don't believe I ever knew him.' He took a few steps back into the room, seeming to be trying to decide what to do with himself.

'He was a writer,' said Koster, frowning.

'Oh, yes,' smiled Wade, eyes on the door. 'Yes, of course —Ring Lardner. Well no, I don't know him either. Who was the other one you asked about?' He peered quizzically at Amsden. 'Terrence Carol? The medicine man? No, I never met him, and I can't think he would have any interest in meeting me. But what can he have to do with this? He isn't a Texan, surely?'

Amsden set his book aside, went to the plate of cookies with what seemed a sudden burst of either energy or impatience, took a cookie—then carried the plate of them to Wade. 'We don't know why we're here any more than you do, Congressman,' he said, 'but from the language used with us, I guess we can assume all the suspects are present —there were supposed to be three, I think. Cookie?'

'No, thank you,' murmured Wade, and looked at his wristwatch. 'I just don't have the time. . . .'

'Mr Koster and myself,' Amsden went on, 'were tossing some familiar spirits around before you arrived, figuring we must share some secret, some connection that made it reasonable for our abductors to want to bring us together. We came up with Terrence P. Carol. We both had the idea Mr Carol might not think too highly of us, although,' he looked around at Koster, 'Mr Koster has yet to make me understand *his* differences with the gentleman.' He faced Wade again, pushing the plate a bit nearer the congressman, giving his head a shake to ask if Wade was sure he did not want a cookie. Then, carrying the plate back to the table, he continued, 'As for me, I'm romantically involved with his daughter.' Setting the plate down, he looked at his own watch and said, 'None of us has the time, Congressman. Maybe we have only minutes to try to gain the advantage of understanding whatever it is about our situations, or Mr Carol's personality, that makes us suspects together.'

Wade gazed at Amsden both circumspectly and sombrely, then said quietly, 'You take this very seriously, don't you?'

'For Christ's sake, Congressman!' cried Koster. 'How can you *not* take it seriously?'

'I've been here since this afternoon,' said Amsden. 'Waiting.'

'*Have* you?' asked Wade softly. He suddenly made his way to one of the wing chairs and he carefully lowered himself into it. 'This could be very serious, of course,' he said to Koster. 'Don't think I fail to recognize that. I still don't think it was just a few drinks that made me so agreeable, and wondered if Rexie My Riddle didn't put a potion in my potion—but I've tried to hope for the best since . . . well, this could be a conspiracy, of course. One can conceive of how this could be happening to practically the whole Congress and Senate, if the timing was perfect—you gentlemen : are you at all connected with the Government? Please be frank. In any capacity it all?'

Koster shook his head. 'No, sir. I'm just a private publisher.'

'I'm less than that,' Amsden said, crossing his arms. 'Just a teacher. And I teach literature, not political science.'

Wade stared at the knot of Amsden's tie, frowning. 'I hope it is not a conspiracy.'

'It isn't likely,' said Amsden, sitting at the sofa once more, 'they'd hope to apprehend every businessman, teacher *and* elected representative of the United States Government, whoever "they" are, Congressman. It seems pretty reasonable to suppose some personal grievance is behind this.'

Koster's nervous eyes were playing on Wade's face. 'Congressman,' he said, 'you suggested Terry Carol might not want to meet you. Was there something between you, then? Can you tell us why he wouldn't want to meet you?'

Wade was frowning and sitting perfectly still. He looked at neither of them.

'Well, I'm not just prying, Congressman,' Koster went on. 'It's no fun speaking with total strangers—Amsden and I have just been suffering from that. But we haven't got *time* for perfect manners. And it really might help us to have some mutual understanding—you can see that.'

Wade looked at his watch and clacked his tongue impatiently. 'My connection with Terrence Carol is very remote. I simply worked on a bill in opposition to granting the public ready accessibility to birth control agencies produced by several firms, including of course Mr Carol's firm.'

'The pill again,' smiled Amsden, taking up the book he had been paging through.

'Naturally,' said Wade, 'there was a lobby in favour of public accessibility, and Mr Carol's firm played a major role in that lobby's activities. I perhaps irritated the officers of that firm when I pointed out one day to the Congress that it seemed to me Carol Pharmaceuticals had a good five or six votes in the United States Congress, but that was only a tactic to caution a few representatives, remind them of their duties. In fact, our opposition was successful and the lobby has since been biding its time. Outside of that, I can tell you nothing—and in fact, all I've just told you is public information. It certainly never occurred to me Mr Carol might have considered me a personal enemy of his, and from what little I know of his reputation, I frankly disbelieve a man of his quality could be involved with what you have called the "kidnapping" of a United States Congressman.'

'Ever the pill,' nodded Amsden, staring into the book with his aloof smile. 'We were just talking about the pill, Koster and myself.' He looked up at Wade. 'Excuse me for not having followed the congressional controversy, but can you tell me why you opposed public accessibility?'

Wade stared at Amsden, then off at the high cupboard. Koster leaned forward as he realized Wade seemed unwilling to answer.

'Congressman,' Koster said, shockedly, 'please—we aren't prying. Both of us, Professor Amsden and myself, we were brought here by force of arms. *Guns!*'

'Oh, well,' sighed Wade, knotting his hands together and crossing his legs as he sank a little more deeply into the chair, 'so was I, Mr Koster—but then, that's the only way to rope in certain old Texans when you want to get 'em to a party. Rexie My Riddle had a gun and a grin for me, so I just said, "You win, ranger!" He liked that enough, put the gun away, and here I am, with no bullet-holes in me. It's the fear of guns that does the damage, you know—not the guns.'

Koster groaned and covered his eyes with his hand. He lowered his hand and looked at Wade with horror. 'Well, *I'm* afraid of guns, Congressman. When that little Chinaman—I was just putting my car away in the garage—and when that little Chinaman poked a gun in my ribs, I thought I'd have a heart attack before he could pull the trigger. I've had two already—heart attacks. I couldn't fight him, I didn't have it in me; so he drove me to a place—in *my* car—to a place where he had his car and we changed cars, then here, and he kept that gun on his lap like he was challenging me to grab it, or . . . now, it may seem like a goddam joke or prank or barbecue to you, but to me it's the real thing!'

'Mr Koster,' frowned Wade, 'you are a very excitable man. No wonder your heart doesn't like the strain. If you'll just calm down, I'll tell you what little I can—which is that, down in Texas, we're pretty conservative people with our ideas about how people should act. It was more than clear to me that my constituents didn't want their children picking up birth control agencies at the corner store—and to be frank, I was very much in accord with my constituents. The existence of a lobby necessitated the organi-

49

zation of a strong opposition, in which I participated. There is really no more to it than that.'

'You're not afraid of guns, but you're afraid of a pill,' smiled Amsden. 'Or is it people with too much constructive as opposed to destructive freedom you're afraid of, Congressman?'

'Amsden, goddam it,' scowled Koster, 'do you have to turn everything into philosophy when for all you know we got exactly five minutes to live? Listen,' he trained his scowl on Wade, 'don't pay any attention to him. After half an hour alone with him, you learn not to pay attention. He's an anarchist. He admits it himself.'

'Ahhh,' sighed Wade, glancing at Amsden, nodding at Koster, finally looking down at his knees.

'And *his* connection with Terry Carol,' Koster hurried on, fastening his scowl to Amsden's expressionless face again, 'is less romantic than just plain messing up his daughter.'

'She messed me up as much as I messed her up,' Amsden defended himself lightly.

Wade shook his head at Amsden, clacked his tongue, then asked Koster, 'And what is your connection with Mr Carol?'

Koster looked abruptly taken aback, opening his mouth before he was ready to speak. 'Well,' he muttered, 'I knew him in school, he . . . had an affair with my sister. We weren't friends, that's all.'

'Sydney's father was going to marry your sister?' asked Amsden.

'What the hell's that to you?' flashed Koster.

'With four minutes to live,' said Amsden, 'I thought I'd inquire. But forget it.'

Koster got his scowl back, but put it on Amsden's knee instead of Amsden's face. Then he looked at Wade. 'He, the bastard, he . . . it wouldn't have been any goddam good, him and me, we just couldn't have got along.' He ran a hand over his eyes. 'Anyhow . . . he hates my guts.

But Jesus, I don't know . . . to see it come to something like this. . . .' He was looking off at the door, now. 'After all these years.'

'Well,' said Wade, 'I find it hard to believe Mr Carol has anything to do with these circumstances, and I still can't help thinking we're going to be in for a rather comical surprise very shortly—not that we're going to appreciate the comedy as much as our host anticipates. A funny thought just occurred to me,' he gazed at Amsden with no humour in his eyes, 'which is that we could have been brought together precisely to antagonize each other. A monstrous practical joke, perhaps.'

'Sartrean Hell,' smiled Amsden, 'yes.'

Wade's humourless eyes returned to Koster, 'You're in publishing, then?'

'I'm Cassius Koster. Koster and Jones.'

'Oh, yes,' nodded the congressman. He flicked his eyes towards the table beside the sofa. 'Those wouldn't be the makings of a drink over there?'

'Just water,' said Koster.

'Water,' mumbled Wade, and he sat back in his chair, his face empty.

'Well, if it *isn't* Terry Carol,' Koster growled softly, 'we've got even more connections hidden somewhere. Unless it's all a big kidnapping heist, and the whole—'

Koster stopped as he heard the lock at the door turning. The three suspects started, Wade leaning forward, Amsden's fingers tensing on the book he held in his lap. Koster's hand slowly moved to his heart.

The door was opened and the three men who had brought the three suspects to the room were now, with still more ceremony than had ushered Wade in, assisting an older man into the room. Behind the four of them followed a woman of fifty-odd years, hair far too blonde and touched with lavender shadows. Her skin had been manufactured in Hollywood and applied with less than perfect evenness—and she smiled with a curious easiness of manner at Harmon Wade as she stepped in after the men, shutting the door.

The fourth man did not look at any of the suspects. He was somewhere in his sixties, and had probably stood nearly to six feet when he was younger. But he looked as if several sicknesses had hammered at him : his broad, square face was at once drawn and sagging, his long mouth was of two heavy lips that were now nearly as pale as his cheeks, his brows were beetling black, hairy, unkempt. He had little of his here grey, there white hair left on top of him. He walked slowly, with the aid of a cane, not—it seemed—to support his accumulation of fat, but because the infirmity of his flesh could only coexist with internal weaknesses. The Negro and the grinning man called Rexie My Riddle helped the newcomer at either side, until he could be seated in the large wing chair opposite Harmon Wade. Then the ailment-ridden old man grabbed in some breath, found a place to rest his cane beside his leg, sat back in the chair and folded his hands over his large stomach. He still did not look at anyone—but abruptly raised one hand and snapped his fingers softly.

'Noreen,' the old man said in his gutturally low, rather retreating and yet arch voice.

'I'm here, honey,' the woman said, and she hastened to the side of the old man's chair.

The man patted the arm of the chair, and Noreen sat down there. Then the man turned his large head and his face, devoid of everything but a record of its illnesses, was touched by the suggestion of a frown. Once again, looking at the door, he snapped his fingers.

The Negro hurried to the door to lock it.

The old man now brought from a pocket his handkerchief, and wiped his mottled cheeks and brow with it, then wiped his nose, at last folding the handkerchief and stuffing it back into his pocket. He sniffed and still seemed unwilling to look at any of the men in the room—all of whom looked at him, now, with varying mixtures of wonder, distrust or awe.

Carson City Go stepped over to stand between the old man and the sofa.

'Boss,' he said, gesturing, 'this is Mr Koster—oh, vely big man, many own connection—him say so !'

Koster winced as he was introduced, pushing himself back into the sofa uncomfortably. He was not sure whether the old man had glanced at him or not.

'This,' said the Chinese, 'Plofessor Amsden—not so important but, oh—vely smart ! Say many thing, all too smart for anyone ever understand; vely smart man !'

Rexie My Riddle had strolled over to stand behind the chair of Congressman Wade. 'Gee,' he said in a phlegmy voice not unlike his employer's, except that it contained more vigour, 'if you don't know *this* fish, boss, should I throw him back in?'

The old man lifted his eyes to look upon Wade. He muttered, 'Congressman,' and suggested a nod.

'Yes, sir,' Wade nodded back. He set his arms along the arms of the chair, sitting more stiffly than before. 'And I know who you are—don't I ?'

'Who is he?' demanded Koster at once.

'Louie Trubel,' said Congressman Wade, both quietly and significantly. 'We've met in Washington—haven't we, Mr Trubel? Or do you prefer your native name, Trubelli?'

Trubel only sniffed, looking at Noreen's thigh beside him. Then he snapped his fingers in the direction of Lancelot Everybody, who came over from the door. The Negro seemed to station himself with curious formality near Trubel's chair, the old man meanwhile wheezing lowly, 'Now you're *my* guest,' nodding slightly without looking at Wade, 'Congressman.'

'Trubel,' Koster muttered.

Trubel lifted his head a little, his eyes darted over

towards Koster without seeming to look directly at him; rather, he appeared to be depending on his ears.

'I'll be damned,' Amsden murmured. 'I've hit the big time.'

Trubel only snapped his fingers again, nodding at the Negro.

The Negro, stationed by his boss, straightened himself and announced : 'First of all, I got to tell you charleys that anything you say's going to be held against you. Next, I got to tell you that if you say nothing, that's going to go even harder on you. Mr Trubel don't have a court of law to work through, so he's done the best he could to organize his own—but Mr Trubel wants to say the laws that work here ain't quite the same as the laws in other courts. Mr Trubel's brung you here as suspects, one of you three charleys being guilty, and we don't have to stay here any longer than it takes to find out which one's guilty. So like, it stands to reason the more helpful you are, the sooner we get our work done—groove?'

Wade, Koster and Amsden stared at the Negro; then stared at each other. Amsden, at length, asked, 'Do we get to hear what the charge is?'

'Man, you groove,' nodded the Negro. 'You betcha. The charge, charley, is murder.'

'Murder!' shouted Koster instantly, even as the congressman frowned with intense displeasure and whispered :

'Murder. . . .' Wade kept shaking his head. 'Mr Trubel—you're going a step further than even *you* better dare let yourself go this time. Well, you may get away with a hundred and ten neat little rackets better than any other gangster of your time. But when you start treating the United States Government like a rival gang—well, you just better be advised : that Government is not a gang, and it's nothing you can set yourself against with any hope at all.'

'Murder!' Koster exclaimed again. 'I'm no murderer, goddam it, and no gangster's going to call me one, *no one* can call me that! What right, what, who do you think you—'

Carson City Go suddenly turned on Koster, smiling, and he leaned down directly over him, Koster quickly taking in his breath. 'Order on court, order court, by Jove,' smiled the Chinese. 'Bad show, Mr Koster. Must not make the contempt of court. Many cost for contempt of court.' Still smiling, he stood erect again and nodded to the Negro.

'Mr Trubel,' said the Negro, 'is merely doing what the law should do but gets prevented from doing by the law. I'm sure you'll all want to cooperate—specially if you want to get home tonight.'

'Oh, now,' Wade said, shifting himself, 'that sounds very like a threat to me.'

'It kind of did, didn't it, charley,' said the Negro.

'Well, I don't know what's on your minds,' Wade said, his drawl deepened by the ponderousness of his tone, 'but I'm a United States congressman, and if you people think you're about to bully me into participating in some kind of kangaroo court—well, even if it's a joke, you have a lot to learn about the kind of men this country elects to its leadership.'

Trubel, his eyes shut, was slowly shaking his head. 'Congressman,' he said in his now guttural, now wheezy voice, 'this room—it's *my* country.' He wriggled his nose, his eyes opened and moved to the Negro.

'Mr Trubel wants to say,' explained the Negro, 'like you three charleys have been extradited, see? Professor, hey— what's a country? Outside of being a piece of land, it's like a collection of ideas—ain't that it? You make the ideas into laws, traditions, so on?'

'That could start a long quarrel and lead to plenty of contempt of court,' Amsden said. 'It's like asking: if we change all the laws and adopt the traditions of anyone but ourselves, what do you call it? If it succeeds, maybe the answer is secession.'

Louie Trubel nodded, mumbling, 'Secession.' He patted Noreen's thigh.

'This room,' stated Lancelot Everybody, 'has seceded from the Union. Mr Trubel's our body of law. The first law I see him pushing is the Great Law of Legal Cooperation, under which you three charleys got to defend yourselves best you can. This is a democracy, so we're all equal, congressmen and teachers and hoods and businessmen, see? So we got no rights of immunity and everyone's—'

'This is ridiculous!' scoffed Harmon Wade.

'It's a goddam outrage!' snapped Koster.

Carson City Go glanced over his shoulder at Koster, which made Koster shut his mouth, and the publisher sat smouldering silently.

'Well, my friend,' Harmon Wade stared straight at Trubel, sitting forward and lifting his voice a bit, 'I come from Texas. And I'm a member of the Congress of the United States of America. No one dictates to *me*!'

'But if little Jack Horner,' grinned Rexie My Riddle behind Wade, 'don't sit nice in his corner, then *who*,' he turned his grin down over Wade, upside down, 'just who do you think is going to pull out his plum?'

Wade snorted, lowered his head and closed his eyes.

Amsden, lighting a cigarette, asked, 'So this murder— is it specific or general? And are you *sure* you picked up the right suspects?'

'Specific and positive, Professor,' said Everybody. 'Any more quizzes?'

'In that case,' said Amsden, 'who am I suspected of murdering?'

'Yeah,' scowled Koster. 'Who'd we kill?'

Louie Trubel patted Noreen's thigh again and looked up at her, making her smile slightly. Trubel sniffed and slowly turned his head to Koster.

'My son,' he said.

Koster and Trubel glared at each other for some seconds, Koster's a glare of anxious astonishment, Trubel's a glare of hauteur and impatience. Then Trubel looked into his lap again. He coughed a few times, sat back and half shut his eyes.

'I never knew you had a son,' Wade told Trubel.

Trubel did not bother to look at Wade.

'That goes against you, charley,' said the Negro. 'That goes against you. You investigated Mr Trubel once, but your investigation took nothing human into account—ain't that it? You should have known Mr Trubel had a son.'

'I think I get it,' said Amsden, abruptly wearing something like the coming of a smile.

'You think you *won't* get it?' grinned Rexie My Riddle, and he winked at Amsden.

'Sure,' said Amsden, drawing the ashtray into his lap and running his cigarette slowly about in it, 'Mr Trubel sees us as American society. I'm education, Koster is business, and Congressman Wade's role is clear. So if Trubel has suffered a loss, he's going to put the whole country on trial. Is that it?'

Trubel sat moving his lips, mulling the idea, his breathing wheezily audible. He seemed near to a smile, like Amsden, and threw his eyes up to Noreen.

'I got the country on trial,' he said. 'Huh, Noreen?'

'You'd be the one to do it, honey,' Noreen answered.

Trubel sighed loudly, suddenly frowned, looking disconcerted and a little sad. He snapped his fingers at Lancelot Everybody. The Negro bent over him and Trubel muttered something.

The Negro stood and pointed at the tray. 'Hey, Carson City—groove?'

'I gloove!' smiled the Chinese. 'Many dlink, I bling,' and he hurried to the tray—pausing before Koster to ask, 'You like humble way China boy hully to serve? I vely lesponsible boy. Maybe if you innocent, get acquittal, you like hire me?'

'Shut up,' muttered Koster.

The Chinese giggled and took the tray to the door,

pointed a finger at the Negro: 'Conviction your lesponsibility,' he said before he shut the door after himself.

The Negro said, 'Responsibility is like Mr Trubel's conviction—like knowing a little bit about the people around you. Is there even one of you charleys who as much as knew Mr Trubel had a son?'

Koster shook his head. 'Not me,' he said. 'I swear it.'

The Negro twisted a smile at the publisher. 'There you go,' he said. 'Like you could've killed someone, and you don't even know who you're killing.'

'How could I have done anything to him if I didn't even know he existed?' demanded Koster.

Amsden asked, 'If you decide someone is guilty—I mean, is the sentence already figured out?'

'Responsibility,' said the Negro, 'that's what courts are all about—right? Ain't that right, Congressman? Like, if I bumped off a charley in your sector and got convicted, man, you know what they'd do to me. Right?'

'It would depend on the circumstances and on the state,' said Wade. 'But I don't mean to—'

'Your answer, Congressman,' the Negro cut him off, 'tells me maybe there're lots of kinds of murder. I groove, man—there *are* kinds and kinds. And one of those kinds murdered Mr Trubel's only son. And one of you's guilty.'

'What if we all turn out to be innocent?' asked Amsden.

Trubel shook his head and the Negro then shook his, saying, 'Mr Trubel's made sure that ain't possible, Professor. If we got to define the word "guilty" to mean "guiltiest", we could do that too—but someone's guilty.'

'Guilti*est*!' said Koster. 'What in hell does *that* mean?'

'Well, it means,' Wade broke in, frowning, 'that Louie Trubel is a vengeful man and, as Professor Amsden suggested, he suffered a personal loss. Well, we are human beings, Mr Trubel, and we—even I, and I am no friend of yours—even I commiserate with you sincerely if you have lost a dear son. But some tragedies, Mr Trubel, just have to be accepted. You cannot hold innocent people accountable, and I know I am innocent; and I believe both Professor Amsden and Mr Koster when they claim they no more knew you had a son than I myself knew it. You didn't know he had a son, did you, Professor?'

Amsden shook his head.

'Of course not,' said Wade. 'Now, if you really wanted to hold yourself up as a man, why, you'd swallow your personal loss like all real men have got to do, and go on being responsible, to use your word; at least, as responsible a citizen as you, personally, know how.'

Louie Trubel suddenly snorted. It might have been a tiny spurt of laughter. He took out his handkerchief, ran it over his nose, snapped his fingers. Lancelot Everybody bent over and listened, then stood to announce solemnly :

'Mr Trubel don't like that kind of story. Mr Trubel likes the kind of story with a strong ending, the ending a man's gut grooves on. Like, Mr Trubel is old-fashioned, he comes from Palermo. Mr Trubel wants to say this room like is part of Palermo now. In Palermo, see, a man does what he's got to do because he's a man—he don't forget that.'

'Yes, yes,' nodded Wade heavily. 'In Texas, it's the same, and I understand; yes, I recall this line of argument from Mr Trubel's testimony down in Washington. And I reminded Mr Trubel then that we all want the right ending, the strong ending—and where it's legal, we struggle after it. And I want to tell you never to stop struggling after it. And only in cases of the direst public emergency can the people dare to take action on themselves. No, now just let me finish—I remind you now, what I just said a moment ago, Mr Trubel : I can sympathize with your loss. But this just is not the proper method to rectify your—'

Trubel, staring at Wade with plain distaste, suddenly emitted a low growl that grew high in intensity : 'Gyaaa*aaah* !' He snapped his fingers irritably. The Negro bent and Trubel whispered. The Negro stood erect to say :

'Mr Trubel says, "Shut up".'

Koster burst out all at once, 'You mean to kill us, don't

you? You're going to kill us? One of us? At least one of us? Come on—say it!'

Trubel's head moved around to face Koster. His mouth bent downwards, so much so that though his eyes were empty, he seemed to be frowning. In a moment he grunted, 'Yeah!' Then, coughing a little, he turned to look at Noreen's knee.

'Mr Trubel says, "Yes",' said Lancelot Everybody.

'I heard him!' snapped Koster.

'Are you saying you're going to kill one of us or all of us?' asked Amsden softly. 'Which?'

The Negro cleared his throat. 'The guilty man will be executed. Summarily.'

'Isn't it possible,' Amsden immediately asked, 'that since none of us seem to know the victim, none of us can be really guilty at all—except in figmentary terms, abstract social terms that—'

'Gyaaa*aaah*!' growled Trubel, disgusted. He looked at Amsden with his down-turned mouth. 'Hey—*shut up*!'

'Mr Trubel,' began the Negro, 'says—'

'He heard me!' The old man snapped his fingers and the Negro bent to listen again.

'Yeah,' said the Negro, rising. He looked at Wade, 'Mr Trubel wants you charleys to understand he took plenty of time to prepare his case. Over a year. Mr Trubel knows one of you's got to be guilty, so we'll make our case—don't you worry. But you can present whatever defence you can manage, and we're going to present the evidence Mr Trubel's investigation produced.'

'You're kidding,' Koster mumbled. Having had his fears confirmed, he could no longer make himself believe in the reality. 'You can't just kill us, kill one of us—it's all, it's—you're crazy. This is some kind—'

There was a knock at the door and the Negro hurried to unlock it and open it for the grinning Chinese, who carried in a larger tray, on which were a few liquor bottles and several glasses, along with a bowl of ice.

'Mr Trubel,' Wade paid no attention to the cheerful Chinese who passed before him, 'this, after all, is something a good deal worse than a kangaroo court, here. I don't know what Sicilian justice is supposed to be, but this isn't only a travesty on legalism : it's a mockery of human decency. A mockery of the very roots of American sensibility. This is a lunatic showcase with your boys and your wife present for no reason whatsoever except to let them see Big Louie humiliating the decent half of American society. Well, you'll be wise to quickly understand I won't be cooperating with you—not at all. If that makes me what you call guilty, then let me be the first to confess my guilt.'

Only Koster was watching Wade. And he stopped watching as the Chinese, beside him, smiled over while preparing Trubel's drink :

'You dlink, Mr Koster?'

Koster scowled shortly at the Chinese, but then blinked, pursed his lips and looked back. 'Yeah,' he said roughly. 'If I could have some Scotch. One shot neat and a double on the rocks.'

Carson City Go giggled and nodded. 'I understand. Can do.'

Trubel had finally looked at Wade. 'This ain't my wife, Congressman,' he said gruffly, before glancing at the Negro again.

'Mr Trubel wants you to understand why Noreen is here,' said the Negro as Carson City Go handed glasses to both Trubel and Noreen. Trubel slowly shook his glass and listened to the ice clink against the sides of the glass. He sipped, sniffled, coughed, then looked at Lancelot Everybody, who was saying, 'This is Noreen Trubelli, Mr Trubel's sister. Mr Trubel had a wife, only she died in childbirth. That was a long time ago. Mr Trubel wanted his sister here for two reasons. She brung up his son, so knew him better than any other person—like, she's a witness. Also, Mr Trubel's got this special regard for a woman's point of view, so Noreen's also a member of the jury. The rest of the jury is the rest of us : me, Lancelot Everybody; Carson City, there; and that's Rexie My Riddle behind the congressman—those ain't our real names, of course, like we're family men with business duties, and you never know the future. Mr Trubel thought maybe we should keep our names to ourselves. Noreen's a family type, too—she married a cousin so she stayed a Trubelli. Her man's a good charley, a terrific family type who just now is down at Leavenworth; he sure deserved better, and he'd've got better if he had a decent jury like us guys.'

Somewhere towards the middle of the Negro's explanation, Koster had begun to mumble, 'Outrageous,' hissing it, whispering it, shaking his head, and as soon as the Negro stopped, he cried : 'This is outrageous!' He snatched rather than merely accepted the two glasses from the Chinese, spilling drops of Scotch on his trousers. He downed the shot at a gulp, handed the tiny glass back and snarled, 'Outrageous! What right have you to accuse us this way? How did you pick us out—by lot? You're all crazy!'

'Mr Koster,' said the Negro, 'you cool it and we'll get the business over sooner and easier—just don't you worry : we'll get our conviction.'

'Oh, you'll get that, all right,' Koster said tautly, glancing beneath his scowl at the Chinese who was affably offering Amsden a drink from his tray.

'No,' muttered Amsden.

'Sure,' said Koster, 'you'll get *three* convictions. Who do you think you're kidding, Trubel? You aren't going to kill one of us and let the other two go. After bringing us this far, kidnapping us, goddam you, I don't believe you mean to let *any* of . . .' Koster's voice broke into a sob, '. . . of, of us go, my God, my wife, my little . . . .' He quickly pressed the cold glass to one cheek, covered his blurring eyes with his other hand.

'Mr Koster,' the Negro said calmly. 'Mr Trubel says two of you will leave. So two of you will leave. Mr Trubel don't lie.'

Congressman Wade abruptly lost his patience and stood up, as if having reached a decision to act. Everyone stared at him. He collected himself for a moment, then said : 'Well—I'm leaving right now. I have to inform all of you that any restraint put against me will bring serious repercussions, and I mean very promptly. I'm going to advise you to let us *all* walk out now, and bring this cruel and illegal farce to its deserved end—it's just the only way you can avoid terrible consequences, Mr Trubel. Consequences to which even Louie Trubel isn't immune.'

Trubel grunted.

Carson City Go, smiling, stopped by the standing Wade to offer him a drink. Rexie My Riddle moved easily around the chair, putting his private grin on the congressman.

'Gee, Congressman,' said the Riddle, 'a chair maybe ain't the most desirable means to an end, but at least it ain't electrified, so ain't that better than a body in a bush?'

'I'm a congressman!' exclaimed Wade. 'You can't—'

'Oh, vely easy kill conglessman these day,' smiled the Chinese as he set the tray back on the table. 'Kill, leave body lay anywhere, cop always look now for political extlemist. Not gangster-type thing to do, kill conglessman. Vely safe for us.'

The Riddle lifted a hand to touch Wade's shoulder.

Wade soon sat down, uneasily, nervously taking the drink from the hand of Rexie My Riddle, as if he thought it was being offered to him. The Riddle's grin widened and he went to the table to take a fresh drink for himself.

Trubel's glowering eyes moved back to the Negro. He mumbled or perhaps only wheezed, his words unclear.

The Negro, staring into his own glass, fell thoughtful briefly, then watched, still abstracted as Rexie My Riddle returned to his station behind Wade's chair.

Finally the Negro said, 'Mr Trubel wants to present the evidence, but as a preface he wants to remind you of his son. He wants you to understand his son. He wants you to grab yourselves some insight into the boy you killed, so the evidence will have some meaning for you charleys. Like, in a way, Mr Trubel's son *is* the evidence. So you got to know him. I don't guess there are any objections?'

Louie Trubel waved his hand to express disgust at the idea that there could be any objection to this manner of proceeding.

It might nearly have been a gathering of friends, or the party Congressman Wade had anticipated, in the deaf view of it: several men and the woman seated informally about the room, drinks in hand, seeming at a glance relaxed enough as Lancelot Everybody introduced what Louie Trubel called a murder.

The Negro's voice was placid, his gestures fluid and easy. Yet if anyone had looked closely, he would have seen anxiety moving upon each person present.

Koster's fingers wandered slowly over his heart while his eyes kept blinking irregularly.

Amsden's tongue moved back and forth between his teeth and his breathing was no more regular than Koster's blinking; he looked more often at Trubel than at the Negro, speaking, as if from some fascination with the gangster.

Wade sat entirely still, except for his eyes, which darted with unexpected suddenness from face to face; and now and again he drew his lips in and shut his eyes—but they would at once open again, to dart suspiciously about some more.

Noreen kept her eyes mostly on the floor, but kept circling one hand about her knee and was given to frequent mournful shakings of her head; sometimes, lifting her eyes, she would find herself glancing at Congressman

Wade and if his eyes met hers, they would dart away the faster.

The Chinese, standing against the wall next to the sofa, kept his eyes hard on the Negro most of the time, but now and then tensed his eyes on Amsden, Koster or Wade, as if to remind himself they were in his charge; his face relaxed from his various performances, the cheer left it in favour of a settled bitterness.

Rexie My Riddle remained behind Wade's chair, arms folded across the top of the chair. From the constancy of his grin he might have seemed the least anxious of all present—and yet it was his very grin that made him seem ill at ease, for it was too resolute, inflexible, something he had painted on himself, a kind of mask; and the more that grin was looked at, the less certainty could be felt that the Riddle knew how to reveal anything of himself. Rather, he seemed ever to be waiting.

Louie Trubel, old and quiescent as he appeared, was relatively mobile where he sat. He would drag his fingers down the skin of his cheeks, touch Noreen's thigh beside him, cock his ear this way or that, move his broad mandible back and forth and lick at his lower lip, cough, and all of his gestures were performed so slowly, stingily, that he seemed more still than he was. His eyes refused to participate in his active attentiveness : they were always his ears he relied upon, and he was always listening—to the Negro, to the breathing of others, to his own wheezing, alert, as if he expected it might be urgent to interpret the least sound about him.

Lancelot Everybody, looking at no one for too long, fidgeting with the glass in his hand as he spoke, was saying :

'Mr Trubel wants to be frankly plain with you. You call him a gangster—so he goes along. Mr Trubel says the occupational nonconformist, he's got to conform a little bit more where he can than your ordinary conformist; he's got to work harder, act better, just to keep himself a place in his neighbourhood—you groove? So Mr Trubel says, okay, call him gangster—but in a way, that means he's a special citizen, or else he wouldn't've lasted so long. Like, Congressman Wade tried to nail Mr Trubel for violence and drugs down in Washington, only he couldn't. Mr Trubel's an honest gangster, and he don't get involved with the families, and the reason he's on top so long is because he don't get involved with feuds, drugs, whores; he keeps clean, he stays with the sports, he gives to charities, he lives like a gentleman because he's a gentleman. But you want to call him a gangster, and Mr Trubel says: okay, a gangster—so Mr Trubel's wife was a gangster's wife. Mr Trubel's son was a gangster's son. He goes to his son's grave, and he's a gangster putting flowers on the grave of a gangster's son.

'But Mr Trubel, he's old-fashioned. Like he holds a family man has responsibilities. You try to make life better for your son than it was for you, never mind what you call professions. Mr Trubel ain't ashamed of his work, but he learned the cost of it. He was damn careful to train his son away from being a gangster—like, this is why, when his wife died, he called in his sister to help with his son. A boy needs a woman. And hell, Noreen, she needed a place too, then. So Noreen became like the mother of Mr Trubel's son, and his son—man, he grew quick, he was rare, he outgrew us. Mr Trubel thought maybe because he was trained like to be anything except what his father was, but he was different all right. He outgrew Noreen, he even outgrew Mr Trubel. Mr Trubel wants to say he knows that. He don't need a college professor to explain that.

'Except we figure the reason the son outgrew his father, like I say, it was because Mr Trubel had these high ideals for his son. It wasn't easy—it was tough: Mr Trubel had to stay out of his son's way a lot, see, because Mr Trubel thought a father should be strict, but he was a gangster and the boy could have interpreted his father's strictness as some kind of gangsterism. Kids are funny, they interpret for themselves. Mr Trubel would think of things like that,

66

so he saw how he himself couldn't always do for his son, like couldn't be the big voice so easy. So he chooses a couple capos—me, Carson City, Rexie—capos he trusts because he knows how we can be strict without getting messy, sassy, fuzzy. He appoints us kind of part-time fathers. In this way, his son's got a big family. Not to say most of the work of rearing him wasn't Noreen's—it was.

'Hey, Amsden—you got a beady light in your eye, there. You thinking Louie Trubel deserted his son? Yeah, charley? Man, you listen : how many fathers would sweat to groove on the things a son studies in all the schools he got sent to? Just so he'd understand his son better when they visited together—huh? But you ask yourself, wasn't Mr Trubel's son ashamed of his father for being a gangster? Look : Mr Trubel wants to be plain with you—there were problems. Only I want to tell you charleys about something Mr Trubel's son said to his father that really grabbed Mr Trubel, he ain't going to forget it. His son said this time, Papa, like nearly everything I learned about right and wrong or wise and stupid, I never learned from you—but like the one thing you taught me, that I never learned from anything else, is so important that without knowing that, man, there wouldn't be no way to use things like right or wrong or wise or stupid. Then his son said, Papa, that one thing you taught me is honesty. Because his son knew Mr Trubel could get called "gangster", but he was plenty honest. Mr Trubel holds that—'

The Negro stopped because Congressman Wade had been unable to restrain a scoffing snort and a shake of his head.

'Congressman Wade?' said the Negro curtly.

'Nothing,' muttered Wade.

'You interrupted the court for no reason?' asked the Negro.

'Court,' muttered Wade with a piece of a grin.

'One hundred dollars for contempt of court,' said Lancelot Everybody.

Wade snorted again. 'It's unbelievable,' he said, and chuckled sharply, looking at Koster.

'Two hundred dollars for contempt of court,' said the Negro. 'You can pay when the hearing is over, charley— and you just keep in mind how you can run yourselves up a real fancy bill quick, if you feel you got too much bullion in your accounts and you want to unload. Of course, since maybe the condemned charley ain't going to have to pay his bill, you could be one of the two who'll have to share that cost, too—so maybe you don't want to encourage too much contempt of court at that. You see how it is.'

The Negro paused to study the tensely baffled faces of all three suspects before continuing :

'So anyhow, Mr Trubel set these standards for himself and his son. Man, Mr Trubel never pretended it was easy studying all them school books. Mr Trubel never had no education at all. But he respects education. Hell, Mr Trubel sent *me* to college two summer semesters, to study economics. Carson City and Rexie both went to night school. One thing they studied was child psychology. That strike you funny, Professor? We took it seriously enough. And Noreen memorized Doctor Spock the way you, Professor Amsden, maybe memorized Langston Hughes or someone important like that—yeah? Well, you got a friend in Mr Trubel : he respects poetry and all that stuff, too.'

Trubel was snapping his fingers, so the Negro stopped speaking and bent down to let Trubel mutter into his ear.

'The thing is,' the Negro said, standing high again, 'Mr Trubel wanted his son to have a noble aim—like, not necessarily to be a priest or anything, but something "holy". "Holy" is one of Mr Trubel's words—only it don't just mean like religious, it—Noreen, honey, you're a woman : what does Mr Trubel mean by holy?'

Noreen sat up straighter, rounding her mouth and speaking the word 'holy' for herself alone. She gazed down at Trubel, blinking, the old man merely examining his own fidgeting hands. 'Louie once said,' she began carefully, but then stopped, squinted, pushed a hand softly against her hair to feel its neatness and found herself gazing at Cassius Koster. She gave him a low giggle and Koster wrinkled his nose distrustfully. Finally Noreen looked at Lancelot Everybody and said in slow measure, 'Responsible . . . unselfishness,' and promptly looked down on Trubel for confirmation of her moral definition. But the old man said nothing and hoarded his attention on his moving hands. 'Holiness,' she murmured. 'Oh! It also means . . . remembering those who went before.'

'Groovy,' said Lancelot Everybody. 'Holiness is responsible unselfishness with a memory—groovy, honey. Congressman Wade's got a sour façade. Man, he can't cut Mr Trubel's idea of responsibility.'

Wade laughed, nodded his head, gestured for the Negro to continue. 'Go on, go on,' he laughed. 'This is better than anything I've seen since Jerry Lewis. Say—who's Rowan and who's Martin here?'

'Contempt of court,' said Lancelot Everybody. 'Carson City, you keeping a record?'

'I never forget!' the Chinese smiled.

'Congressman Wade's behind three hundred dollars,' said the Negro.

'Check!' smiled the Chinese, writing imaginary numbers on the air with an imaginary pencil at which he licked. 'Hey! I no give testimony—no one ask *me*?' He pouted comically in the direction of Trubel, who sniffed up some permission for the Chinese to address the proceeding. Smiling more widely, Carson City Go stood away from the wall.

'I talk about Mr Tlubel son,' he said, 'because maybe you get idea flom black fliend how that boy is too simple—plain boy. No! Him stlange, him vely stlange, mystelious boy—have gleat seclet in soul. Like him say once to me, Carson City—minute man bleak faith with self,' the Chinese snapped his fingers much more efficiently and quickly than Trubel might have, 'then soul become without memoly. And poor poor man, him not even know piece missing flom soul. Vely mystic boy, vely stlange. One time Mr Tlubel son say to me, Carson City—my fliend command to me, come! we find happy fleshman girl, many happy good lay time we make, these day girl at college is eating-bird and vulture-boy fly, oh, fly quick,' the Chinese waved his hands absurdly in the air, but no one except My Riddle grinned at his antics, 'fly down on fleshman girl, Mr Tlubel son say she not know she got to live all life with even one night—so open arms and such like, give boy-joy many time.' His comic nature pasted a ridiculous frown onto his brow. 'Why it hurt Mr Tlubel son if he too have happy time? He don't know! But he have instinct that warn him, and he no do unless he sure he do good. Mystic boy. Plohibit self flom easy joy. Too good? Maybe so! Maybe so!' Smiling, he bowed to Amsden, then leaned back against the wall again—his smile, curiously, fading into bitterness again, his eyes losing their pointless cheer. Only noting the change in his face brought awareness that the Chinese played a game comparable to the Riddle's grin : he refused to be himself in this room.

The Negro was saying, 'Carson City's telling you Mr Trubel's son was a citizen. He *wanted* to be a citizen. He had quality. That's the point, charleys : he had values. So maybe like Carson City says, he was too good, like it was a weakness. Me, though—I'm going to say the quality of the son grooved along with the quality of the father. I'm going to say—'

'I can't stand it!' Cassius Koster suddenly shouted. They all turned to him and he moaned smally, then scowled at the Negro. 'What's it all about? Why are you doing this to us? Tell me what you think I've done, let me defend myself, my God—I'm going to have a heart attack and die before you accuse me!'

The Negro gazed dourly at Koster for some moments before intoning, 'Fifty dollars.'

'Fifty dollars,' rasped Koster, his voice low and quaking.

'Fifty dollars . . . Christ's sake,' he pulled out his wallet, his hands shaking as he dragged paper money from it, spilling it on the floor, 'take it, take it, but stop *torturing* me like—'

He was interrupted by the angry rap of Louie Trubel's cane against the floor. Trubel was glaring coldly at Koster, and Koster's lips twitched so meanly that their ends leaped deeply into his cheeks. He moaned and sat back, eyes shut.

Trubel glanced dully at the Negro.

'Well, Mr Koster,' the Negro said as imperturbably as before, 'you give some ear-attention and dig how this has all got to do with you. Like, if someone's got values and don't stick with them, man, you got like you call an unstable situation. Like, if you don't use your values on your own kind, you ain't got any loyalties, so you know what you are? Man, you're nothing. Or maybe a Playboy playing the anarchy field, like Professor Amsden. Because, man, if you run something—a company, a government, whatever—and your values stink, man, you're a teacher teaching *everyone* to stink like you. That plain enough?'

Amsden had murmured, 'Jesus,' in something like awe as the Negro spoke, and Lancelot Everybody looked at him coolly for some moments—as if uncertain that he had spoken at all, and if so, wondering whether he should be charged with contempt of court. Presently the Negro proceeded :

'Mr Trubel wants to say, like, the top's got to set the example for the bottom. You run something like a company, just out for the take and cutting it for yourself on all sides, man, that ain't no business—that's bareass anarchy. Just like Professor Amsden's—except he's open about it, so don't feel the need to set no good examples at all. Bad ones do fine for him. Or like the yellow rose of Texas, there, he's got some weird idea how you use symbols instead of examples. So if someone don't get mucus all over his vest at the sight of a flag or the sound of a bugle, he's what you call a lousy citizen—he's disloyal. And the representative of the people, there, he can be a pig all he wants, because it's the flag and the bugle setting the example—not him.'

'You son of a bitch,' muttered Wade, eyes pulsing hotly, 'I'll—'

'We ain't going to talk without producing evidence,' the Negro cut him off, 'so don't make speeches yet. You'll get your chance. I *am* a son of a bitch, as it happens, Congressman, but if I wasn't I'd get you for contempt of court. But don't bug me again, because we got to move on and my background's got nothing to do with this hearing. Now I'm going to skip some years—only, you keep it in mind this was a big close family that Mr Trubel's son belonged to, you keep it in mind we had our own idea of holiness. Keep it in mind we had some ideals and figured it was worth while pushing Mr Trubel's son out into *your* world, charleys, where we figured ideals counted for something. Keep it in mind he was a cheerful kid. Keep all that in mind, and I'll skip on a ways—like, to when Mr Trubel's son was eighteen, Professor Amsden. That's when he went to Kingston College. That's when he got to be your student.'

Amsden stiffened, his eyes fast on the Negro's, seeming to labour to try to recollect if he had ever had a student named Trubel.

'Noreen,' said the Negro, 'she's the one can tell you how Mr Trubel's son got changed. He changed a little bit, Professor—after getting the word from you. You know? Listen, Noreen,' he turned on her, as she was slowly sliding her legs from the arm of Trubel's chair, 'let's have some feminine testimony, honey—and remember how Mr Trubel cautioned you. Tell us how Mr Trubel's son changed after he started at Kingston? What'd he learn up there? What'd he tell you?'

Noreen, her head down, stood up and shook her head slowly, looking from the floor over to Amsden, at whom she suddenly smiled. Amsden blinked back at her. 'I'm no *oraytor*,' she announced too loudly, 'but I promised to try. I mean shit, I don't get it myself,' she giggled at Amsden uncertainly, 'why it is you hate goodness. I guess all those writers who write the books in your course, shit, they—'

'Noreen!' Trubel mumbled, a harshened wheeze.

She whispered down, 'What, Louie?'

'Language,' he mumbled. 'This is a court room.'

'Yeah.' She looked back at Amsden, her face abruptly saddened with chagrin. 'I don't talk good,' she began again, softly. 'I mean—I mean, like all those writers who write the books for your courses, we read that stuff, and what confused us is—I mean, shit, we couldn't figure out why they hate everything so much. Why they hate people— you know?' Her eyes fell. 'I guess they're all smart and new, but shit . . . I mean, those writers, shit, how can they hate people so much? Well, I mean . . . shit . . . everything changed—'

'Noreen!' Trubel glared up at her.

'I'm doing my best, Louie,' she frowned. 'This is my best.' She put the frown on Amsden, then on the floor. 'Anyhow—after my boy started in at Kingston, gee, just *everything* changed, Professor. Honest.' She glanced somewhat imploringly at Amsden, seeming to ask him to take away the small smirk he wore, as if she were cowed by his teacher-nature. The smirk stayed there and Noreen bit at her lip and lowered her eyes. 'It's true,' she murmured. 'All he'd ever talk about for a long time was Professor Amsden says this, Professor Amsden says that. You're a good teacher, okay—like, it seems you don't just talk: you want to listen to the student. And somehow that makes your ideas stronger. But shit, your ideas—shit, you made him think about things all over again. The whole notion of good and bad got lost somewhere, because, shit, he had to be bad to be good, of all dumb things. Like in a way, you *want* murder, that's the thing that just startled us. Shit, even *murder* can be good. I mean shit, you—'

'Language!' scowled Trubel.

'Oh, Louie,' she whined.

'Your language stinks,' Trubel said.

Noreen muttered, 'Oh, balls,' irritably, but then she looked sad. 'I'm sorry, Louie.' She sighed at Amsden. 'I mean shit, you call Louie a gangster, but he never preached murder, not to anyone—or all those other . . . shit, those other freedoms. Shit. It was like only bad could make things good, and people who acted right just made things harder for people who—'

Amsden interrupted, 'You aren't making *my* life any easier with *your* methods.'

'Fifty dollars,' announced Lancelot Everybody.

'Fifty dollar, Plofessor Amsden!' called out Carson City Go.

Cassius Koster, shaking his head miserably, slowly bent over and began to pick up his fallen bills of money. Noreen stood waiting to see if the interruptions of her testimony had ended, then put her eyes briefly on the ceiling, considered, and went on :

'I was the one to see the change first. Tommy and me were so close,' the moment she uttered the name, Trubel's hand lifted and dropped, a kind of flinch; while Amsden's eyes glazed over, his vision seeming to retreat into some underconscious in search of a Tommy Trubel among past students, 'like he was my own son. I mean, shit, he *was* my son. Shit, he had no other mother—just me. He knew how to hurt me, I knew how to hurt him, we both had our faults. He wasn't all that good, like Carson City says, that maybe he wasn't human. Shit, he was human. Talk about language, shit—he could really fly off the handle,' she glanced uncomfortably down at Trubel. 'I mean shit, Tommy talked and wrote distinguished, like a scholar or something. But shit, talk about bad language if he got *mad*! But shit—he *wanted* to be good, that's where the mysteriousness of his character comes in : he really wanted to be good, like he valued rightness as some sort of special objective or something. Shit, though, he was human, he could hurt and get hurt. But what happened to him up at Kingston,' she shook her head just once, looking more evenly at Amsden, 'that wasn't just hurting him. Shit, Professor—that was like killing something inside him, down so deep inside he couldn't even live without it. I mean shit, when you taught him everything had to just *die*, just stop and end, especially everything a kid would think was decent, you know? I mean shit—how could you think that wouldn't include *him*? Don't you think you should *know* people? Don't you—'

'You haven't the—' began Amsden, the Negro stating instantly :

'Fifty dollars.'

'Fifty dollars !' echoed the Chinese, writing on the air.

'Just wanted to compliment the little woman for lifting the judicial tone,' muttered Amsden.

Noreen stood blinking unsurely at Amsden, seeming near to apologizing with her eyes for the cost of interruptions. 'All I mean,' she said, '—you were his idol. Maybe you never even knew it, because he was shy and quiet—but you must have known he was a good student. You must have noticed him special because, I mean shit, you *knew* him. He thought you were brave, like you were standing alone against the whole world or something. The way you'd talk, everyone was against you and you were the only one telling kids to do all these things, drugs, sex, all these— shit, Professor, nothing's wrong with wanting kids to *stand* for something, like Louie said once while we were investigating you, but shit, don't you ever discriminate? Like, if all the things that are good are bad, and all the things that are bad are good, shit, all you do is turn things around and you don't discriminate any more than anyone else.' She shook her head. 'Encouraging your own girls, I mean finding boys for them,' she shook her head and shoved her lips out at Amsden, 'shit.'

'Just doing my bit for the coming generation,' sighed

Amsden, who then snapped out in unison with the Negro:

'Fifty dollars!'

'Shit,' mumbled Amsden.

'Fifty dollar!' cried the Chinese, making a mental account.

Trubel mumbled, 'It's a court room, Noreen.'

Noreen hissed at him, 'You want me to talk or not?'

'Talk,' mumbled Trubel, closing his eyes. 'Talk.'

'The thing is,' Noreen began soon, 'the only thing *you* left Tommy to believe in, Professor, the only thing he could inherit from the past was death itself. Shit, people *need* the past, Professor. You cut it away, and shit—what do you expect to get that's better than—oh shit, I don't know. It just didn't make sense to us, like, to say the way to make things right when some things go wrong is to make everything bad and start all over. Shit, that don't use any imagination. We—'

'Sometimes that's the only way to *fifty dollars*,' Amsden interrupted himself, frowning at the Negro, and went on, '—the only way to make things right, Mrs Trubelli. You ruin a recipe in the kitchen and how do you separate the flour and milk? No—you throw them both away and start all over.'

'Shit, Professor, it's *my* kitchen!' cried Noreen, while Trubel was taking up his cane to rap angrily with it on the floor, Noreen rushing on: 'Shit, *you* can't come in and tell me *my* recipe's going wrong, and he was *my* son, and since when do *you* get to vote for everyone else, or like my husband always said when he was home, when was *you* ever in the fuckin' navy?' She frowned down at Trubel.

The old man was suddenly in a cold rage that made him cough instead of speak. He coughed, rapped, glared at Amsden, coughed, rapped loudly and after choking on his coughing he finally managed to say, to the counterpoint of sharp raps of his cane:

'You—don't—throw—people—away—like—garbage!' He nodded, glared a second more, then wheezed in a whisper,

'Professor Amsden.' He sighed or grunted, then sat back and carefully set his cane away.

After a silence, Noreen returned her eyes to Amsden—they were sad once more—and she resumed her testimony: 'I mean, it was crazy. Instead of wanting people to be happy, it seemed you wanted to throw everyone away like shit—happy people, wretched people, everyone—just start back with the monkeys or something.' She paused briefly, watching Amsden, as if expecting him to object. He only sat still, frowning tightly, toying with the book he had kept in his lap. 'So anyhow,' Noreen continued, her voice growing louder again, 'he had this friend up at Kingston. His best friend. Shit—some friend. His name was Drake, and he had money and everything—I mean he was what you call "quality", not "quality" like Lanny meant, but sort of attitudes and outlooks you get reared with in wealthy families. He and Tommy liked to argue a lot about things, like the things Professor Amsden would talk about. He'd bring his girl with him and sometimes they'd just talk for hours, Tommy usually trying to explain your ideas, Professor. I think more for himself than for Drake, because Drake didn't really care about the ideas so much. It's funny, like if you get reared with attitudes instead of ideas, Tommy said, they start to seem like ideas. That's what Tommy said, but shit—Drake didn't need to understand the Professor because he kind of lived like that, anyhow. He just thought the Professor took life too seriously. In fact, Drake kept trying to get Tommy in bed with his own girlfriend, and shit, I could tell from everything Tommy said, she was ready to seduce him. I guess because he was a virgin, see, and some girls want to prove something to themselves that way—like before, boys took pride in getting girls like that, only now it goes both ways. Well shit—Tommy was weak, like Carson City says, and he was foolish to take her so seriously, he was dumb to take sex seriously—I mean shit—but it went with his character, and he did, and I never understood it, but it's funny . . .

77

I understood *him*. It was *right* for him. He was frank with me and wanted me to talk about it, but I felt Louie or Lanny or someone should do that. I mean shit—Drake would say, what's the difference, shaking hands or kissing or laying, you know? Shit, so you have skin on skin, that's all, whatever it is. *I* never took it so seriously, but Drake couldn't pin Tommy down on it, because shit, he had this idea there was the *meaning* of intimate things that was important—you understand? Oh shit, *I* didn't know what to say,' she giggled, a weary giggle, and for some reason glanced from Amsden to Harmon Wade. 'Shit.'

'Aw hell,' muttered Trubel.

Noreen blinked down on him. 'What's the matter?'

Trubel glared up at her and wheezed. 'Contempt. Fifty dollars.'

She kept blinking at him.

'Fifty dollars,' said Trubel. 'Your language stinks.'

Her face reddened right through her cosmetics and she hissed: 'Shit, Louie—you never made me pay for saying *shit* before!'

'Now I did it,' Trubel muttered, lowering his head.

'Shit on that,' she said angrily. 'I won't pay.'

'Look, Noreen,' Trubel said lowly, turning his eyes up. 'I won't pay!' she said more sharply.

'Okay, okay,' Trubel wheezed furiously, waving a hand at her. 'Testify.'

Noreen, frowning, her tone a grumbling one, started again: 'So I sent him to Louie, and Louie said it *didn't* matter if he went to bed with girls, like he could go to bed with every girl at Kingston, smart girls, dumb girls, what the hell—only, he should remember one thing: like, if he didn't have any conscience, you know, never mind, forget it, it didn't even matter if *he* stayed alive, because a kid with no conscience had no contribution to make; but all the private things he collected about him in his life, all that was going to stay with him, if he had any conscience. It didn't matter if it was something private, or public, he'd have to take it to bed with him all his life, keep it in his soul. Or else live without a soul, like—you know? Cynical. So Louie said, Tommy—you better be sure you go to bed with girls you'd be proud to share with your wife, because she's got to go to bed with them too. So Tommy said, Hell, he didn't guess that kind of girl would go to bed with him at all. So Louie nodded and waited awhile, then he just said, that's tough.' Noreen smiled down on Trubel, pushed a hand at her hair, then smiled at Amsden. 'I thought that was real good, though of course it never answered really for Tommy. I mean shit, he couldn't be sure good wasn't bad anyhow, and he couldn't be sure smart wasn't dumb. He thought like Drake's girl was Joan of Arc or something, helping Professor Amsden take society apart—see? Poor kid . . . he was pretty frayed.

'So then, sure, I mean . . . shit, she seduced him, all right. He couldn't get her off his mind. Shit, he couldn't get her out of his bed, even. Shit, it was like a massacre. He wasn't sorry at all because, shit, he figured he had conquered something in himself; like some obstacle had prevented him from doing things, so he could never really make a contribution to people the way Professor Amsden wanted people to. He went around even happy for a while, saying, I'm liberated, I'm liberated! Shit. I mean, not to me—that was to Rexie, he said that. But Rexie told us. Wasn't that what he was saying, Rexie?'

Rexie My Riddle widened his artificial grin and looked at Amsden. 'He got liberated, like,' he confirmed in his gravelly voice, 'so wasn't he free, Professor? Wasn't he liberated? From people? Ain't he now?' He gave the grin back to Noreen.

Noreen brushed her hair back, smiled at the Riddle, took in fresh breath and continued : 'Shit—he was the one doing the chasing now. So she succeeded with him. Only, shit, she lost interest and one day she found out this son of some New York actor was going to another college and she got interested and took out after him. Tommy couldn't believe it. Shit, she not only wouldn't marry him, she mocked him. He'd told her how he was the son of Louie Trubel to be honest with her—shit, he had to hide that usually, it got too much attention—but that girl, she just said, me marry the son of a gangster? Only shit, he didn't blame *her* for that. He didn't blame his teacher. Shit, no. Shit, he just came home and disowned Louie. Yeah. It turned out the gangster hadn't made him tough enough for the civilized world out there. He disowned Louie and he disowned me . . . then went away.'

The sudden sharp rap of Trubel's cane against the floor punctuated Noreen's conclusion, and Trubel dragged his cold, arrogant eyes over to Amsden and glared. He said nothing and at length shifted his gaze to Cassius Koster.

'Mr Koster,' Louie Trubel grunted.

Koster started.

'Mr Koster,' said Trubel. 'What do you think of a teacher like that?'

Koster glanced at Amsden, at Lancelot Everybody, back to Trubel. He shook his head slightly.

'Mr Koster,' muttered Trubel insistently.

Koster said lowly, 'I open my mouth and you'll charge me.'

'Mr Trubel's asking you a question,' said the Negro. 'There's no charge on answers.'

'I mean,' said Koster, and could not think what to say. 'I mean . . . you take it so significantly. But every kid gets into jams with girls. It sounds like your son was . . . very sensitive, so he,' Koster shook his head, 'had a tough time adjusting. It's a pity he couldn't have met, you know— some other kind of girl.'

'What do you think of a teacher like that?' Trubel persisted, throwing his eyes briefly to Amsden, then back to Koster.

'Of course,' Koster said weakly, 'Professor Amsden already knows I don't agree with his ideas, but . . . .'

Trubel shook his head and would not be refused : 'What

do you think of people like that? A teacher like that, a friend like that, a girl like that—that's some college, huh?' He kept glaring at Koster. 'Mr Koster—what makes people like that?'

Koster nodded quickly. 'You write me a book telling me that, I'll give you an advance of fifty thousand dollars.'

Trubel went at the floor with his cane again, his thick brows collecting angrily over his eyes, his mottled face purpling. He snorted gutturally, 'I don't want your fifty thousand dollars! I don't need your fifty thousand dollars! I don't write books! Koster—listen: what made Trina Koster like that? Huh?'

Koster's face paled, then darkened and he started to tremble violently. His shaking hand went to his heart—and abruptly, before the Negro could grasp him, he leaped all the way from the sofa to Trubel's chair, diving atop the old man with a furious gasping. The Negro at once took him from behind, pulling him off with such force that Koster had barely touched Trubel, and he was swiftly hurled back to the sofa.

'You stay sitting, charley,' said the Negro, bending menacingly over Koster. 'You hold your bottom to that cushion, charley, and you keep quiet.' The Negro breathed heavily, angrily, as if the attack on Trubel represented a genuine heresy. 'You sit steady, charley, and you think of something: Mr Trubel wants you to think how he could have had your daughter here tonight instead of you. Only you blame the top, not the bottom—groove, charley? Only Mr Trubel wants to find out from you what tricks you used to cut a freaky girl like that. See, your girl's alive and she's going to stay alive awhile, ain't she? Only Mr Trubel's son, he's dead. And he's going to stay dead awhile. Mr Trubel wants to find out why.'

Koster's face still trembled, his eyes shifting between burning vividness and filmy dullness, wrath and with- drawal, till suddenly his lips quivered and his eyes filled with tears. When the Negro stood away from him, Koster drew himself into the corner of the sofa and seemed to want to isolate himself from the others in the room. Turning his face as far around as he could, covering his face with his hands, he quietly wept.

Trubel patted the arm of his chair, nodding at Noreen. She, trembling a little herself, lowered herself beside Trubel.

'Mr Trubel,' Congressman Wade said softly, 'what you are doing is very cruel. It is unnecessary, and very very cruel.'

Trubel gazed vacantly at Wade, wheezing. Soon he said, 'Amsden took my son's faith. Koster's girl took his hope. Congressman, you gave him a reason to die.'

Congressman Wade narrowed his eyes sharply.

'I give this testimony!' Carson City Go said abruptly, getting his silly, false smile back on, standing free of the wall again. 'I enjoy addless important man! Like Confucius, addless self to political plopliety of Conglessman Wade famous Four Bombs Ploposal.' He bowed with his silly smile, at Wade, and said, 'Hello! I charge you with murder!'

Trubel intruded, 'Wade.'

The congressman put his thin, hot glare back on Trubel.

'Me,' said Trubel, 'I could appreciate that idea : the Four Bombs Proposal. Yeah. I'm a gangster.' He chuckled privately, shut his eyes, waved a hand generally at the Chinese.

'Mr Tlubel gangster,' smiled Carson City Go, 'know many kind gangster business. Four Bombs Ploposal, same like old plotection game. Lose plestige in stleet is bad if even one store say no to you. Same philosophy with,' and the Chinese jocularly crossed himself as he spoke the name, 'Alphonse Capone, namely : must not lose, bad for image, business go bad. So must get tough and more tough, like Conglessman Wade say. Like Four Bombs Ploposal : if first bomb don't make people see you big power in this

neighbourhood, maybe tly new bomb, like you call defolia-
tion. Scare people good. But maybe not enough, so all
same you go to number thlee bomb, cover nation with
napalm, all city with napalm. Must work! Vely bad, vely
stlong! But maybe don't work. So go to bomb number
four, namely, bomb based fission of hydlogen atom—
oh,' he shook his head slowly, 'vely effective! Total bomb,
so soon is nobody there to scare no more, vely victolious!

'Mr Tlubel understand. But Mr Tlubel son, long long go
when he first hear about Four Bombs Ploposal, he too
simple boy to understand, he vely hollified. Funny boy,
him like twenty-year-old, but him dare tlust own mind
instead of wise Congless-mind of Conglessman Wade.

'Oh, them good day, vely good day, for Conglessman
Wade. Him a big storm in Washington. Him aflaid civilian
people got too much power, him aflaid maybe some political decision being made outside Pentagon, so him make
big storm. Get many attention, many attention—many
interview, television, and people begin see how not to think
like Conglessman Wade is same as not to salute glolious
flag, so maybe best thing is to bomb. Many say Four Bombs
Ploposal best way to end things. For example, end war.
For example, end peace. For example, end world. Make
Plofessor Amsden vely happy, I think: end world. Then
Plofessor Amsden don't got to be bad boy no more. Vely
stlange him oppose Government!

'But Tommy Tlubel, him on outside. Him on outside
with favolite girl. On outside at Kingston College because
not know how to act, what to join. On outside flom home,
because him send bad disownership-letter to Mr Tlubel,
saying him tired to be gangster's son. Tommy, though, he
come to me one day—hey, Carson City, him say, you
dlive me to national capital? I say, why you ask poor
China boy do long-time thing like that? But I say, okay,
because I think maybe is good to keep eye on Mr Tlubel
son, him in many stlange mood them day. Not cheerful
no more.

'So I tell Mr Tlubel what I do, and he say, go ahead. I dlive our boy to national capital and him go see many patliotic sight. See Mr Lincoln, Mr Kennedy, see—'

'Tommy Lincoln!' exclaimed Amsden all at once.

Carson City Go kept on, 'see Mr Jefferson, I stick with him best I can, but him mystelious boy, stlange boy, many stlange mood. Go out of motel to walk sometime, not want to talk. Then I wake up next morning, him gone. Just gone. I look evelywhere, I call boss, I say Tommy go out when I sleep and I lose him. Him not have much money. Oh, I wolly! Him in sad mood, him look like big tear-dlop that got spilled, it got legs, big tear-dlop walk alound tlying to evapolate. China boy now vely sad, oh yes.'

The Chinese all at once lost his smile and gave Amsden a sharp look, then turned to Wade and repainted the pointless smile on his mouth, crying: 'Never mind! *I* find out where Tommy go! Sure! Him go to stleet outside your office, him sit down with sign him made, sign say: Not Four Bomb, Not Thlee Bomb, Not Two Bomb, Not One Bomb, all in vely tiny letter, but in vely huge letter it say: No Bomb! Clever sign he make with boxes he find, so it stand by self. Then he pour gasoline on own young body, he light match and say goodbye world! He burn to death there, and Conglessman Wade watch flom window—vely entertained, I think.' Again the Chinese lost his smile, and this time gave his harsher look to Wade, while Amsden was murmuring:

'Tommy Lincoln—Louie Trubel's son?'

Trubel rapped the floor with his cane, rapped heavily, as he turned slowly to Amsden. But then he faced Wade and nodded and said heavily, 'Louie Trubel's son.' Beside him, Noreen ran a hand over her eyes and seemed determined to keep her face devoid of emotion.

'I forgot,' Amsden said so softly he might have been feeling reverence. 'I thought he . . . in front of the Pentagon.'

'No, no,' Carson City Go got his smile back again.

'Blanch office only. Conglessman Wade office.'

Amsden looked dumbfounded. 'But Tommy Lincoln, how could he have been your. . . .' He stared at Trubel in plain disbelief.

Trubel dragged his eyes over to Amsden. 'Yeah?'

Amsden shook his head and said, 'He was so gentle, so completely mild, nothing like you, he . . . when he did that, when I heard about that, even *I* cried. And I don't cry.'

Lancelot Everybody said thickly, 'The jury better make a note of that. Professor Amsden cried when he heard Tommy Lincoln was dead.'

'He was the kid who burned himself to death?' asked Koster of Amsden, his hand on his heart.

Wade had covered his brow with one hand and he said quietly, 'Mr Trubel, I very sincerely regret what happened to your son. Now, I must tell you—the reports that attributed certain callous remarks or gestures to me were far, far from the truth. I can assure you no reporters were in my office. It is true I watched your son die from my window—I am human, and I was shocked, I could hardly pretend I cared so little I was blind to what was happening. But my thoughts were far from what they have been represented as being.'

Trubel issued a long, wheezing sigh and sank back farther in his chair, his eyes peering quizzically about, from Carson City Go, to Rexie My Riddle, to Lancelot Everybody. He gave a just perceptible nod.

The Negro came over to stand by Trubel's chair again, saying, 'Mr Trubel wants you to understand he spent a lot of money investigating. Most of it was spent on you, Congressman Wade, because you were the best hidden. But it was a pretty good investigation, man, and we found out like everything there *is* to find out about you. Including how you got elected, including—'

'Don't you dare!' hissed Wade, bright red, and he might have leaped up, except Rexie My Riddle had him from behind again, mouth wrapped in his hand. Wade struggled briefly, then sat still.

Lancelot Everybody went on, without having blinked an eye, '—including why you got appointed, including details about where plenty of your money comes from, including what you do with it, including what you get out of your congressional relationship with the military, with the armaments industry, charley, and a little debt you got to the National Rifle Association; *and* including a few gifts one of which was a woman you managed to use for a week or so down in New York City, the lure of whose name was no little help in getting you here tonight. A few less sparkling gifts along the way, and oh man, ain't *you* been busy in your own name? Mr Trubel wants to tell you something, charley: no matter who's convicted here, we know you can walk out that door, and we just ain't going to worry. You ain't going to talk to anyone, not you—not even if we execute our murderer in your lap, in case you ain't the guiltiest murderer yourself. Charley—we trust you.'

Wade sat fuming, clutching the arms of the chair, looking as explosive as Koster had ever looked. Every time he opened his mouth to speak, however, Rexie My Riddle clamped a hand over it. From his corner of the sofa, Amsden chuckled nervously.

'Yeah,' the Negro nodded, significantly, 'we trust you, charley. We took time to be sure we could trust people. Mr Trubel took time preparing for this night. Like all them books over there, Mr Trubel read them. All of them. He don't read so fast, like he had no education, I told you —so he took his time. He wanted to understand things before we got here. He wanted to know you charleys, and he wanted to groove on his son, so he read all his son's books. All them books,' the Negro gestured towards the cupboard, 'they were Tommy's books. This room,' he swept his hand around slowly, 'this here used to be Tommy's bedroom. Yeah.'

86

The announcement caused the three suspects to shift uneasily and take a fresh look around the room. Amsden was the only one whose curiosity seemed greater than his uneasiness : his eyes glinted wonderingly on objects, even on the ceiling, as if he wondered how Trubel's son had felt when there was a bed in the room and he lay upon it staring at that ceiling.

'All them books,' said Trubel, nodding at Amsden. 'The only one I liked was these Russian stories.'

'Chekhov,' murmured Noreen.

'Yeah,' said Trubel, blinking at the Negro.

'Mr Trubel wants to say he read all the books in your course,' said the Negro, 'because you were his son's teacher, and—'

'I didn't have any Chekhov in my course,' said Amsden.

'No,' said Trubel. 'The books in your course—they *all* stank.'

'Mr Trubel believes like people are in special situations,' the Negro started again. 'Like a teacher, for example. It's like my own job was with Mr Trubel's son, sort of : a part-time father, a *mind* father maybe, something like that, so it means a kind of responsibility. Only, all the stuff you taught, it was like lessons in how to forget all about relationships and responsibility and maybe even forget there *is* a mind in the body. Like, the whole mind gets directed into how to make life a little better for your own body. Like this cat who makes just having a sexual orgasm into a whole ideal, which like Noreen says is going back to start with the monkeys again. Man, I mean I ain't no genius, so you got to explain this for me. Mr Trubel wants you to save yourself by teaching us what you taught Tommy Lincoln. That way, see, maybe we'll go right out and burn ourselves, and you'll be saved. Teach !'

Amsden squeezed the book in his lap and shook his head in defiance. 'You know I can't teach you to do that, any more than I taught Mr Trubel's son to do it.'

'Listen, charley,' glowered the Negro, 'you taught Mr

Trubel's son why tomorrow ain't worth the getting to. That was like showing him a map from Kingston to Washington. According to you, according to your books, charley, we got to dismantle the world and start all over. We're giving you a chance to convince us. Go on : teach !'

'Screw you, Sir Lancelot !' Amsden burst out madly. He looked at Trubel, bitterly. 'Look, if I'm going to teach contemporary literature, I have to teach the contemporary literature that exists. It's based on ideas, and the ideas get inspired by what *is*, not by what isn't. To teach those ideas, I have to understand them. You're right : there's plenty of destruction in the works these days—but that's because there's plenty that doesn't work, that deserves destroying. Look at Congressman Wade, over there ! But I fight these things my way, and I'll be frank to say I'm damned sorry Tommy Lincoln fought them *his* way, because he was wrong. You get someone on your side, you need him alive, not dead, and I wish Tommy Lincoln was alive. I admired your son a great deal, Mr Trubel. And I enormously regret he couldn't comprehend contemporary ideas without becoming obsessed by some of their darker tendencies. But I don't see how it's my fault.'

'Only *we* figure,' the Negro retorted, borrowing some of Amsden's sudden brittleness of tone, 'it ain't a teacher's job to try to get ideas to lead a good life—that's backwards. Ideas got to help people lead a good life.'

'No,' Amsden shook his head firmly, 'you're wrong. A teacher isn't a wet-nurse. Students have to learn the ideas. You don't alter the ideas to conform to over-sensitive students.'

Louie Trubel rapped at the floor with his cane and wheezed at the Negro, 'Structure !'

'Mr Trubel wants to say,' the Negro announced, still looking at Amsden, his eyes and Amsden's arrogant on one another, 'he couldn't make his business work without a structure. Like, you don't make nothing work without structure. Like, ideas that don't fit into a structure your

88

students groove on, they float away; but the students got to fit into a structure, too, or *they* float away. So the teacher, he's got to make ideas and students fit into the same structure, or he ain't got ideas and he ain't got students and no wonder you got anarchy, because without structure you got nothing, nothing to be loyal to, so you got no loyalties to teach except to your own pale corpuscles, charley.'

'And if the only structure you have to be loyal to is so rotten it needs anything but loyalty?' flashed Amsden.

'Then, charley, I don't know—you're the teacher,' the Negro nodded, 'but I guess you got to point to a better structure, or just get out of the teaching business. Mr Trubel's idea is that in an organization, too much loyalty to yourself is disloyalty to the structure. That's like saying, you teach what *you* teach, and you got no loyalty to anything at all.'

'I'll tell you something, Sir Lancelot,' Amsden said, his tone still brittle. 'If Tommy Lincoln was alive and here right now—he'd be on my side. Not yours.'

'Yeah?' scowled Trubel turning more quickly than seemed comfortable for him to face Amsden. 'You think so, Professor? Teach me. Teach me why!'

Amsden shook his head. 'It's useless,' he muttered. 'It's impossible.'

'Because,' said Trubel thickly, 'I don't think you got solutions, Professor. I think you only teach love of problems.'

'Mr Trubel,' Cassius Koster broke in, his voice a moan, 'you aren't giving us a chance.'

Trubel's eyes moved coldly over to Koster.

Koster contorted his face into misery and said, 'You're not giving us a chance. First you send your boys out to scare hell out of us, kidnap us. You suddenly give us the story of your son's life. Then you say one of us, or all of us, killed him, and we have to defend ourselves, meanwhile charging us every time we talk too much. When do we get to catch our breath? When do we get to think? Don't we get to prepare a defence—I mean, Christ, even for thirty minutes? Professor Amsden's right: this is impossible.'

Trubel gave his attention to his fidgeting hands.

The Negro asked Koster, 'What you got to think about?'

'I mean,' said Koster, 'even the commonest criminal,' he bit his lip quickly, glancing at Trubel, before rushing on, 'he not only gets a lawyer, he gets plenty of time to prepare his case. Your court, my God—it's impossible. Your idea of justice has hung us already.'

Trubel took out his handkerchief and slowly dabbed with it at his brow, then ran it across his mouth and put it away. He glanced at the Negro, as if for an idea. The Negro only gazed back at him. Trubel looked up at Noreen, and she merely looked as if she were trying to weigh the application.

Trubel grunted and turned his eyes to Rexie My Riddle.

'Am I an *answer*, boss?' grinned the Riddle.

Carson City Go said, 'Long tlial, much work. Why they need time? They don't tlust us, is my idea.' He frowned at Koster.

Trubel snapped his fingers softly and the Negro bent down to listen to him.

Then Lancelot Everybody rose, and proclaimed: 'This hearing's adjourned for thirty minutes so you charleys can cut a defence.'

Koster, as if he had been acquitted, sighed and shut his eyes and seemed to relax a bit.

While Rexie My Riddle and Lancelot Everybody were helping him to stand, Noreen standing over him—as if to console him should he be dropped—Trubel was saying, 'You guys talk. It's okay. I'll tell you something. I got patience. I waited a long time. You want thirty minutes, Koster? Okay. I come back in thirty minutes—*I'll* be thirty minutes more ready.' He nodded at Wade. 'Congressman,' he said, 'hey—I got more evidence. I been careful. Real legal.'

The Negro helped Trubel at one side, Rexie My Riddle at the other, Trubel still finding security in depending on his cane as he moved with Noreen to the door, which Carson City Go was holding open. At the door, Trubel turned sideways, poking his head back towards the suspects. He glanced around the room.

'Yeah,' he muttered, 'year ago, this was Tommy's room. I could hear him walking around, sometimes. When I was downstairs.'

The old man put his head down, coughed and finally let himself be helped away. Carson City Go shut the door after them, locking it from outside.

The suspects sat still for some seconds, then, with tentative eyes, wordlessly, they glanced at one another.

TWO

Wade sat back, scratched his brow abstractedly, squinted around at the window and sat back still again with a great long sigh and a whisper of, 'Oh, God. . . .'

Koster, too, was squinting, his eyes worrying from Amsden to Wade. He said softly but tensely, 'We don't have much time.'

'For what?' said Amsden, looking at neither of them.

Congressman Wade leaned forward, elbows on legs, staring at the floor, then took up his glass from the floor and rose. 'Well,' he said, 'everything they're going to tell us, you know—it's just lies and confusion.' He went to the table to mix himself a drink. 'There's not much we can do about it, Mr Koster. You can't establish a defence when you have that kind of jury. No. The first thing we better agree on is simply that we're on our own side. And not on their side.' He glanced pettishly at Amsden. 'I'm afraid I think that is very important.' He kept his pointed glance on Amsden for a few seconds, then asked, 'Can I get you a drink, Professor?'

'I don't drink,' muttered Amsden.

'Mr Koster?'

Koster nodded remotely, 'Thanks.' He picked up the roulette wheel and gave it a vicious spin. 'Congressman,' he said, staring at the wheel, 'is Trubel serious?'

'Scotch?' asked Wade.

'Thanks,' said Koster.

Wade pouted as he poured, then said, 'He's a gangster, Mr Koster. If he has a sense of humour, he hasn't displayed much of it tonight. These bottles give me a Texas-size thought,' he formed a rather grave grin as he handed Koster a glass. 'We ought to take one each, break them, each of us choose a thug—'

'No!' exclaimed Koster. 'My God—that little Chinaman, he'd just take the bottle and fix me with it. Don't ask me to fight, Congressman.'

'I suppose I'm no longer young enough to do the job, myself,' said Wade. 'Though it would afford me some consolation to put that little yellow hood on the floor where he belongs.'

'Now, that's constructive thinking, Congressman,' nodded Amsden. 'That's good old Four Bombs thinking, calculated to kill us all.'

'See here, I don't need *your* advice,' Wade frowned, setting the Scotch away and recorking it, taking up his own glass. 'Anyone who thinks like you, Professor, why— I'm inclined to have thoughts about him not so far off Louie Trubel's.'

'Oh, look,' Koster said hoarsely, 'please—let's not quarrel. We don't have time for it. It seems to me Trubel expects us to end up attacking each other, and like you say, Congressman, we just have to stay on our own side.' He looked beseechingly at Amsden. 'No matter what happens, I propose we all stick to one easy rule : defend each other, even if we aren't sure we like what we're defending. Do you agree, Professor?'

Amsden, instead of answering, stood and stretched his arms wide, then walked to the window.

'I agree with Koster,' Wade addressed Amsden's back. 'I'd only add : the best defence is no defence at all. Silence.'

'Right, I agree,' said Koster. 'I mean, we just don't *have* to lower ourselves to a sort of gladiatorial spectacle for the entertainment of Louie Trubel. I don't—I'll be blunt—I don't have any intention of arguing with either of you or any of them about my little girl's behaviour or private life. That's flat. I'll take that up with her when I see her. And I agree with Congressman Wade : Trubel's throwing a lot of bunkum at us, he's just trying to fix guilt and blame on us because he can't face his own part in losing his son. And I'm not falling for it. I think I know my daughter better than Louie Trubel, and I frankly doubt she ever knew his son.'

Wade nodded, saluted Koster with his drink, walked over to stand by his chair, again addressing Amsden's back. 'Nor am I about to let Louie Trubel use this kangaroo court to ridicule either United States policy or an elected representative of the people of Texas. And *I* hope, Professor Amsden, you aren't about to let a gangster force you to defend the ethics of your profession in a disgraceful situation like this.'

Amsden said nothing for some time, facing the window. At length he answered quietly, 'His ideas do interest me.'

'Oh, no,' scoffed Wade, and Koster scowled and sighed.

'I don't guess he could alter my reasoning,' Amsden went on, still refusing to face them. 'Hell, I have to live with my own mind. But . . . it's fascinating—listening to the whole outsider, Louie Trubel, looking in at society and, in his own way, trying to make legal sense. *Moral* sense.' He turned with part of a smile twisting his mouth. 'Prepared to write the whole social scenario, if he has to, to make his sense work. In a way, you know, I see where Tommy Lincoln got some of his stuff—I mean, there's something of the solid old world about Trubel. Something he's still loyal to. I mean *really*. Inside himself.' He nodded, lifted a hand to examine his nails or knuckles. 'In a way, I admire him.'

'Well, that surely is the most foolish declaration,' Wade stated irascibly, and he took a large sip from his glass. 'What the hell does it *matter* what his ideas are? The *fact* is—he's a gangster. Why, everyone knows that. And if what he says is true, *this* gangster is also a traitor to his country, for he has taken pains to investigate a representative of the United States Congress *only* to construct a series of malicious fabrications against him and that, I think, dishonours the country.'

'Are you going to report his treason in Washington?' Amsden asked coolly.

'What do you mean, Sir?' asked Wade.

'I just asked, is Trubel right or wrong? He doesn't think you'll talk to anyone even if he lets you go. Are you going to report how you were kidnapped? Are you going to haul him down to Washington for his treason against the Congress, for example?'

Wade's mouth hung open, aghast. 'Do you mean to stand there and tell me,' he demanded in a voice like quiet thunder, 'that you *credit* his lies about me?'

'All I asked was—'

'Just a minute, just a minute!' shouted Wade, colouring darkly. Too flustered to speak for a minute, he only held his hand to his throat until he had regained his composure, then said, 'We had just better go back to the beginning, here. Do we or do we not agree to unite our defences and refrain from *attacking* each other?'

Koster glared at Amsden. 'We got to! This is no game, you know, Amsden.'

Amsden shrugged.

'Well, all right, then,' said Wade, still not having rid himself of some ruddiness. He drank quickly, ran his palm over his mouth. 'We should also agree that silence is the best defence.'

'Louie Trubel, as you keep pointing out,' said Amsden from the window, 'is a gangster. Maybe it's just Hollywood's influence, but I'm a little scared to be too altogether cagey. Rumour has it, gangsters have special ways of making people talk.'

Koster was instantly alarmed. 'You think he would torture us?'

Amsden faced Koster with his derisive smile. 'Mr Koster —he's going to *kill* one of us. Why should he care if you die slow?'

'Oh, God,' moaned Koster, knotting his hands together, then reaching out for his drink only to find the glass empty. He stood quickly to pour himself another. 'I won't be able to take that. I've already taken too much.' He swallowed Scotch, poured again. 'The old ticker's going to give out,' he promised as he sat down again. He gave Wade a solemn nod.

Wade, now sitting on the arm of his chair, said, 'Sure . . . it's a possibility he'll blow up. He's a psychotic, we'd all agree to that. So silence might get to him, he might use violence. But let's at least agree on silence while it *can* be maintained. If it becomes outright physically impossible . . . okay, we just better start praying. But till then, we shut our mouths. It's like the military, after all : you're a prisoner of war, so you give your name, rank and serial number. I guess they got enough details already, so we don't owe them any more.'

Koster had taken to shaking his head morosely and he was not looking at Amsden or Wade, looking nowhere in general, but somewhere in his remote mind he heard, and gave a small assent of, 'Agreed.'

'Professor Amsden?' Wade turned his head over, looking at Amsden severely, as if he expected to be rejected.

Amsden turned to the window once more. 'But can't we at least try to talk Trubel out of the whole sideshow?' he asked. 'Or even, if it comes to that, turn the tables on him and try to prosecute him?'

'Prosecute *him* !' exclaimed Koster, looking over in horror.

'Well,' said Amsden, turning back, 'you're the one who said he was responsible for what happened to his son.'

'Yeah, sure,' said Koster, sputtering a bit before going on : 'But you're talking about a madman ! We don't want to get him any more worked up than he already is.'

'Mr Koster is right,' said Wade. 'And what you suggest is not really proper, Professor. It would admit a kind of propriety to the very absence of the judicial process. We are between us no more a legal body than Trubel and his cohorts. We can't deny his right to try us on the one hand, then proceed to try him on the other. No—we're no jury. I think we have to agree to that.'

'Agreed,' said Koster quickly.

Amsden shook his head disgustedly, took his breath in, raised his upper lip and exhaled a whistle. 'It seems damned sad to me to dismiss what could be our one active hope. I mean, the fact is, Trubel *is* more responsible for the death of his son than we are.'

'He is *what*?' asked Wade, eyes wide, voice strained. 'I'm afraid I don't understand that language, Professor Amsden. I don't want to think you are saying we *are* in some way responsible for the insane act of the son of a madman?'

'I didn't mean that,' Amsden mumbled, '. . . not directly.

'Not even *in*directly !' snapped Wade.

'Hell, come on,' said Amsden, leaving the window to cross the room slowly, 'you can't know such a thing straight off the top of your head. Ideas *do* motivate. Besides—I knew Tommy Lincoln, and his interests were on a rather simple, moralistic level. He wasn't insane, Congressman.' Amsden still had his back to the others, but now faced the books, peering at titles again. 'It's queer as hell, though— one thing you just couldn't have said about Tommy Lincoln was that he cared about political forms. I never knew my anarchy hit him so hard—or I did, whichever; but I can see how, if it *did* hit him,' he turned, 'it couldn't have been very promising, since there was one kid who never could have lived by my recipe. But he wasn't a political type, which is something I thought of when I read how you, Congressman, promised an investigation to learn just what was the connection between burning Buddhists of the Vietcong, and the boy who died in front of your office. He wasn't a communist, if it interests you.'

'I know that now,' said Wade. 'But you can surely see how it was necessary to investigate that. It could have been very important.'

'Well, you were wrong,' snapped Amsden. 'He was politically unsophisticated.'

'All right, all right,' Wade waved a hand, impatiently. 'The boy's death disturbed you. You cried, didn't you? Is that what you said? Only, you didn't go out and burn your body, did you?'

'What's that got to do with anything?' asked Amsden.

'It simply means,' said Wade, 'you might not have agreed with my philosophy, but you weren't insane. You didn't kill yourself over it.'

Amsden bent his head and looked gloomy, stuffing his hands into his pockets. 'When I was a kid,' he said, 'I had all these big ideals. Very big. Then I grew up a little and learned how ideals are for kids.' He looked at Wade. 'Tommy never grew up. He believed. Not only that—he was that kind of simple kid who honestly believed *others* would believe, if you only showed them right and wrong. A very simple kid—almost ordinary; except he didn't have the fair share of ego most of us get.'

'We're wasting time,' said Koster. 'I think we ought to just agree on basic things—like it needs a certain kind of individual to pour gasoline over himself and make a bonfire out of his living body. If you can't see that, Amsden, you're blind.'

'I *can* see that,' said Amsden. He looked down again. 'Yeah.'

'Okay, then,' frowned Koster. 'And it isn't really anyone's fault, not even his father's, so far as I'm concerned, if a kid does something that extreme. Surely that's agreeable !'

A curt nod of the head from Wade, who said briskly, 'Absolutely !'

'Funny,' muttered Amsden, whose head still hung. 'If

Tommy Lincoln was here now . . . if he could see the three of us together : me, the Congressman, you,' he looked at Koster, 'his father, the whole scene—you know what he'd do?'

No one cared to ask, so Amsden turned back to the books, muttering :

'He'd become an anarchist.'

'I don't care what he'd become,' said Koster. 'He was a nut.'

Amsden swung back around, his tone brittle once more :

'Either one of you might have polished yourself off, yes, maybe a year or two ahead of Tommy Lincoln, with his collection of thoughts, breaks, ideals—and neither of you would probably have taken the trouble to believe enough in nobility to think there was something noble left to die for. The fact is, right now, you're so goddam worried for your lives that you don't care any more that Tommy Lincoln is dead than you did when you saw it in the papers —or you, Mr Congressman, when you saw it right out your window. People who don't care, Mr Congressman— what in hell are they doing down in Washington, anyhow?'

'Or to put it another way,' said Wade, 'why should you be a teacher, Amsden, when you don't give a damn about students, only about yourself.'

'Maybe you're right!' snapped Amsden, deepening his frown. 'Or you, Koster : why should you be empowered to decide what books people will or won't read, when you don't give the first part of a damn how your own life or any individual life is affected by—'

'*Give a damn!*' shouted Koster, his mouth twitching in aggravation. He looked outrageously stupefied for just a moment, then shouted again : '*Give a damn?* You wonder if *I* care if that kid's dead? Goddam it, Amsden, I'm *glad* he's dead ! That's the only piece of news I've heard tonight that brings me some relief. Trubel's son is dead ! Thank God for *that* ! Because if he really *did* seduce my daughter, and I got out of here at all, and he—'

'Seduce your daughter!' exclaimed Amsden.

'—and he,' Koster blustered on, 'and he was still alive, I'd—yes, goddam it, seduce my daughter! If my daughter was touched, I don't need a gangster to try to pin it on her. I know my girl! If something like that happened, no one's going to tell me it was her fault and not the fault of a gangster's son! My God! The mere thought makes me so goddam mad—that he even *touched* her! Don't ask me, now, to care if he's dead, or worry about what the dirty little bastard died for. Just thank God he's dead!'

Wade had quickly moved over in front of Koster, lifting his hands, trying to calm Koster's spleen. 'Please,' he was saying, 'please, now, Mr Koster : this is exactly what we must not do. If we can't dismiss fighting amongst ourselves here, now, without Trubel and his hoodlums in here to antagonize us, well how are we going to keep from fighting when they're right in here on top of us, prodding at us?'

'Okay, okay!' Koster cried. 'Only, this goddam intellectual baby-chaser isn't going to say anything against my daughter, goddam him, or I'll kill him too!' He looked, for all his paunchiness, as tightly drawn as a bow that might fire at Amsden when he moved so much as the muscle of a finger. Wade's anxiously undulating hands at last captured his attention, and Koster, cursing in a whisper, sat back, slapping a hand over his eyes.

'Believe me, I understand your feelings, Mr Koster,' Wade said, and turned on Amsden with a remonstrative sigh. 'Professor, we just beg you to cooperate with us, even if there are ways in which you can't agree with us. My understanding was, we were voting on matters in a democratic spirit—and if two agree, then we adopt a motion as practice.'

'Look,' Amsden shot straight back, 'I've already told you I'll clam up, if that's the decision—but stop telling me to *think* like you think.'

Wade shook his head, retreating to the arm of his chair again. 'Good Lord,' he muttered, 'we'll convict each other before Trubel ever gets around to us.' He glanced at Koster, but the publisher still had his eyes covered; so he turned to Amsden. 'I do think we must agree that the line of defence we have to pursue is to presume that the boy's *nature* was directly involved—*most* directly involved—with the way he chose to die. I think we are otherwise agreed to restrain ourselves from either testifying against ourselves, or attacking each other. In the event of violence— well, all I can say is, we must do what we can to stick together.' He shifted his eyes over to Koster again as the publisher dropped his hand to his lap. 'If we hold them off by plain courage in the face of cruel interrogation or even force—well, you know, I think we may find ourselves, in the end, in some kind of bargaining position.'

'Except,' said Amsden, 'it's hard to believe they really mean to let us go.'

'Well, they *said* they would let two of us go,' said Wade. 'And I just suppose our main purpose is to try to make them let *three* of us go.'

Koster sighed and took up his drink again, glowering into it sadly. 'No,' he mumbled, doom-eyed as he turned to Wade. 'Amsden's right. They aren't going to let us go— not after all this.' He shook his head, touched one eye with his finger, sipped Scotch. 'No. We're dead men. My poor family. You don't know what a shock this is going to be to my family. They need me.'

'Well, I have a wife too,' said Wade. 'Thank God my sons are grown and married, but my wife would be left alone at fifty-four, and don't think I'm not feeling that, Mr Koster. But I think there's a chance we'll make it out of here all right. Consider that Trubel is a sick man—sick enough to arrange this entire outrage. That sickness is the sickness of a father's passion on the death of his only son, and for my part, you know, I can actually comprehend the nature of that passion. I believe I can sympathize with that. And *this,* Professor Amsden, is perhaps the one argument we can safely pursue : we understand his wretchedness, we sympathize with him even though he failed to sympathize with us. We can allow ourselves, in deference to his deep feelings, a pledge of silence, if he simply cuts off this horrible masquerade and allows us to leave. We can offer him that honourably, don't you think, Mr Koster?'

Koster did not look excited by the idea. 'Sure,' he said, 'there's nothing wrong with that, only . . . well, I don't guess Trubel is going to be moved by that plea.'

'Perhaps not,' said Wade, 'but if we repeatedly make it abundantly clear we're not about to join him in this farce, and if we are calmly resolute in taking this one generous attitude and facing him with it—well, you know, it might take on an increasing validity for him. Now, isn't this agreeable?'

Koster shrugged out a nod.

'Amsden?' asked Wade, but before Amsden could reply, the door was suddenly being unlocked and pushed open.

Lancelot Everybody, Carson City Go and Rexie My Riddle all came into the room burdened with cargo. The Negro carried an object whose nature was at first difficult to determine, a long cylinder on a frame of some sort—but the nature of the object was easily enough deduced by the cargo that followed: a folding table, brought by the Chinese, and a heavy projector of some sort, embraced by the Riddle.

'Don't mind us, charleys,' the Negro said, moving to a wall of the room where he began to unfold the portable film screen he carried. 'You still have a few minutes.'

'We had,' Congressman Wade huffed, rising from the arm of the chair, then sitting on its cushion, 'thirty minutes granted us, barely enough to catch our breaths in, much less to compare our reactions to this masquerade. I see your word is no more reasonable than your method.'

'Talk, charley,' shrugged the Negro, adjusting the

frame's screws to secure the screen in a standing position. 'You go right ahead, don't you pay no attention to us. You don't want to be too strict about the defence anyhow, Congressman—might give propriety to our version of the judicial process, man.'

Wade opened his mouth, seemed to gasp and again his cheeks coloured. 'You have wire-tapped us!' he charged furiously.

'Vely tlue!' smiled the Chinese. 'Confucius, him say what good for goose, vely pleasant for gander. Goosey government wire-tap us, we wire-tap you. Open society. Bang bang!'

'All set?' the Negro asked the Riddle.

'Ain't I smiling?' returned the Riddle, who was.

'Do we go?' asked Carson City Go.

The three went to the door where the Chinese turned to bow to the suspects, which inspired the Negro and the Riddle to imitate him—they all bowed; and copied the Chinese again as he pointed a finger at Koster, the Negro pointing at Amsden, the Riddle at Wade, all intoning soberly: 'Bang bang.'

The Chinese giggling, they shut the door, leaving the suspects alone again.

As it was after their earlier departure, for a time the suspects were still. Koster kept glancing about the room, as if trying to spot the hidden microphone.

'They're a bunch of nuts,' Koster whispered nervously.

'It's a lunatic asylum, all right,' said Wade.

Suddenly, Koster—his eye on the books in the cupboard —seemed to decide that was where the microphone must be, and facing that way, he cried: *'Bastards!'*

'No, that's no use,' said Wade. 'I guess talking is out. We may as well just sit and think.'

For several moments they might all have been doing that, till at length Koster muttered, 'All I can think of is epitaphs.'

Amsden said softly, 'Here lies. . . .'

'My poor family,' moaned Koster.

'We'll be all right,' Wade said half-heartedly.

'Here lies,' Amsden said again.

'You suppose,' asked Koster, 'they'll let my family have my body?' He looked from Amsden to Wade.

'Why not?' said Amsden. 'What would they want with it?'

'I hate the idea of my family not taking care of my body,' said Koster.

'Here lies,' Amsden mumbled still again.

'Can't you cut that out?' Koster glared at him.

The three fell into a deep, long stillness during which none looked at another, all seeming to maintain an inward focus. Koster's hand jumped to his heart, fell quickly back into his lap when the door opened again.

The Negro, the Chinese, the Riddle and Trubel's cane all helped the old man back to his chair, in the same shuffling silence that accompanied his first entrance. Noreen minced in behind again, shutting the door after the men. This time she kept her eyes down.

Trubel, as before, looked at no one; and, as before, once he was settled he took out a fresh handkerchief and ran it over his face.

Amsden uncrossed his legs and shifted his posture, to sit more erectly, as if recognizing a formality that needed observing in the simple return of Trubel to his son's room. Meanwhile, Rexie My Riddle had restationed himself behind Wade's chair, Carson City Go sat between Amsden and Koster, and Noreen resumed her place on the arm of Louie Trubel's chair.

'I would like to point out,' said Wade with quiet resolution, 'your agreement to allow us thirty private minutes in which to consider among ourselves was premeditatively and arbitrarily false, our conversation *not* being private and our debate interrupted before the conclusion of the allotted period.'

Trubel sniffed and fidgeted. He moved in his chair and

drew from a pocket a large pocket watch. He consulted with this watch for rather longer than seemed necessary, his pale, broad lips mumbling inaudibly. He glanced quizzically at Wade, as if still not having been able to make clear to himself the meaning of Wade's language, then wheezed a sigh and looked at the Negro. 'Lanny?' he said lowly.

Lancelot Everybody nodded, and gestured Rexie My Riddle to the projector on the folding table. 'You better see if the shots are lined up, Rexie.'

'You have photographic evidence against us?' asked Amsden of anyone in general, looking at the projector.

'Well, we call it that, charley,' said the Negro, watching Rexie My Riddle, who quickly glanced through a series of slides, reinserted them into the projector, then switched on the projector. He directed a sudden beam of light, brighter than the room light, onto the standing screen.

The Negro wandered over to the lamp table, holding his hand on the lamp switch as the Chinese, striding to the door, turned off the overhead lamps.

'Rexie?' said the Negro.

'Ain't I smiling?' asked the Riddle.

The Negro turned off the lamp, leaving the square of light upon the screen the only illumination in the room.

'We ain't got no movies,' said the Negro, 'only some blow ups, like family snapshots. We got millions of pictures of Tommy, but we ain't got time to show more than a couple. We'll do our best to get you to know him,' he promised in the darkness, as the projector's slide mechanism clicked over and abruptly, on the screen, there was the intensely cheerful, joyously frivolous face of an infant, perhaps three years old.

The light in the infant's eyes was spectacular enough, seeming to be pressed out of some soul-centre of gleeful abandonment: obviously, the infant accepted the camera that was taking a picture of him as some formidable tease and was challenging it, or its possessor, to explain its nature, which was bound to be comical.

'That's Tommy at three and two months,' said the Negro. 'Like we say, he was cheerful—even when he was big as a sack of potatoes, he was pretty likely to have that particular grin on his puss. He never completely lost it. Thought it might cheer you charleys up to know Tommy was cheerful while he existed outside your orbit, at least. Let's have another, Rexie.'

In the unclear light falling from the beam of screen-light, Amsden caught the brief dart of a glint off Koster's eye. Koster might have been thinking to ask what purpose was being served with the family snapshots. On the screen, the infant image was quickly transformed into that of a small child, five or six, smiling in a way that suggested some strange perplexion : it was as if the same child had merely and too abruptly grown older, but still expected, somehow, to understand the by now strange mystery of the camera box so frequently held before him.

'Professor,' the Negro said in the darkness, 'you're a teacher. Tell us something : ain't that a cheerful kid?'

The eyes of the child were thinner, but still bright. Not now so much with abandonment as with childish bewonderment, that settled on his face like an aura of prettiness. Yet, he was not a specially pretty child : his nose was snub, his cheeks plump, his hair straight and cut too short. He did, at any rate, look cheerful, and the Negro again asked :

'Professor, was Mr Trubel's son cheerful, there?'

There was no reply—but then, suddenly, there was a short series of low thudding sounds, and a sharply irascible hiss of, 'Goddamit!'

'Carson City!' snapped the Negro, angrily. The Negro himself had the sofa lamp on before the Chinese had the overhead lights on—and Amsden was seen to be kneeling on the floor near Koster, who lay stomach-down on his elbows, scowling at Trubel, then at Amsden. Wade set his hands on the arms of the chair, peering at the two open-mouthed.

'You nut,' Koster muttered to Amsden.

Trubel sniffed and looked away. He might have been amused or bored. The Negro had strolled over to look down while Amsden managed to get back to the sofa.

'You two charleys get kind of independent in the dark,' remarked the Negro.

'I didn't know he was there,' was all that Amsden could muster that soon as a defence. He glanced disconsolately at Koster. 'You okay?'

'Yeah,' whispered Koster, rubbing one hand. 'You stepped on my hand, is all.' He cleared his throat, glanced up at the Negro, back at Amsden. 'I figured you were,' he looked up at the Negro again, 'someone else.'

'Where you go to get by Go?' asked the Chinese from the door, holding up a key for Koster's inspection.

Louie Trubel watched with a vague curiosity as Koster crawled back to his place at the sofa, then turned to Amsden : 'Professor.'

Amsden took in his breath, picking up the book he had been toying with, holding it tightly again.

'You knew my son,' said Trubel. 'You didn't find him cheerful?'

Amsden only looked worried—and soon leaned over to whisper something to Koster.

'Answer *me* !' demanded Trubel, scowling. 'Why answer him? You planning again?'

'I wasn't planning anything,' said Amsden, sitting back.

'What did you say to him?'

'I was just wondering if I should answer your question.'

Trubel thought about it, blinking slowly. 'Why?' he asked. 'Is he your lawyer?'

'Mr Trubel,' interjected Wade softly, 'if I could just remind you what you already know. You already overheard our brief conference, so what I'm about to say, I say only as a matter of courtesy—maybe I'm pretending you honoured our privacy in order to shelter whatever modicum of respect I might entertain for the order of what is happening here. In any event, you know perfectly well we don't wish to speak in our own defence at all. We feel it would be futile and degrading, under the circumstances. You also know already we are able to fully sympathize with the deep sorrow you have experienced. Obviously, it has been very traumatic for you—but there is nothing dishonourable in suffering. It simply means you loved your son. Well, we comprehend that hurt. We even comprehend how you have allowed your passions to overwhelm you, leading to this excess of passion over reason. It is in sympathy with that, as again you have already heard us agree, that we're very willing to offer our sincere pledge of silence about this strange affair, if you simply bring it to its end now. As Professor Amsden pointed out to us, there *is* something of beauty in the old-world sensibility your loyalty to your son displays, and perhaps this increases our own comprehension of the compassionate involvement which has brought us all to this unfortunate night. With this in mind, I assure you our understanding guarantees that you can trust our pledges of silence very completely.'

Trubel's scowl had vanished and he sat watching Wade, chewing the air silently, a small frown coming and going, coming and going, upon his brow—as if he worked to fathom not only Wade's statement but the motivations that had inspired it. He suddenly sniffed, sniffed again, reached for his handkerchief, and his mouth began to twitch. His eyes shot up to Noreen, and he seemed to have to labour to hold his mouth still; and then he shut his eyes tightly, but he could not hold it : clots of thick, deep, gutturally rumbling, slow laughter coughed free from his throat and he carefully buried the laughter in his handkerchief. Carson City Go began to giggle in little spurts, Rexie My Riddle widened his grin to genuine proportions, the Negro kept rolling his mouth around a small chuckle, and Noreen—shaking her head slowly at Trubel—wore a small, sad smile. Trubel seemed to choke on his laughter, pushed his face forward into the handkerchief, then took up his cane and began to rap on the floor with it—whether for attention, or to help himself regain his breath, it was difficult to tell. The suspects looked with a consternation like quickened fear at one another, then at Trubel, then at one another again.

Gradually, Trubel's laughter subsided and he snorted a few times, looked with wet eyes at Noreen, dabbed at eyes and brow and cheeks and mouth, glanced at his handkerchief, shook his head slowly and replaced the handkerchief in his pocket. He coughed, resettled himself carefully, could not resist one final amused twitch and snort and only then —slowly—did he manage to bring his face back to its wonted vacancy. And only when he had managed that did he look again at Congressman Wade. He snapped his fingers. The Negro bent over, nodded and then stood and strode to the door and out of the room, the Chinese locking the door after him.

'Congressman,' said Trubel, sniffing, 'say—what's your salary?'

Wade was colouring again. 'Well, I don't think that is your affair.'

'Why not?' muttered Trubel, eyes on his own lap. 'I'm a citizen.'

'Are you?' asked Wade. 'I didn't know. It's hard to tell, from the way you act.'

Trubel sniffed a bit more and fidgeted, and glanced at the door. Still looking at the door, he said, 'I can account for a hundred thousand dollars you spent last year. Can you?'

'I don't have to hear this!' cried Wade, slapping an arm of his chair.

'You're a rich man,' said Trubel.

'I have investments,' Wade retorted, 'yes. And that is a very legitimate way of earning returns in this country.'

There was a sharp rap at the door and the Negro was

already returned, Carson City Go admitting him and once more locking the door. Lancelot Everybody carried a portable telephone with a long cord, whose end, towards the projection table, he plugged into an outlet, then stretching out the long cord so that the telephone could be placed in Louie Trubel's lap.

Trubel, as he lifted the receiver and worked the dial, opened and closed his mouth, as if exercising his muscles for the call he was about to place. 'Hello,' he said vaguely to who was evidently the operator. 'I want the Attorney-General's office in Washington.' He waited. 'No, someone'll be there tonight . . . yeah.' He waited some more, his mouth opening and closing, his eyes staring off at nothing

'One good thing,' Wade said softly, staring at the telephone. 'They'll be able to trace your call.'

Koster and Amsden gaped astonishedly at Wade. Wade only passed his hand over his eyes, then loosened his necktie.

Trubel nodded slightly at Wade before glancing at Koster. 'Mr Koster,' he said. 'That's your Government.' He looked off at nothing again, then said into the telephone, 'Hey, honey—never mind. Mm—never mind. I'll place the call later. Later, yeah.' He put the receiver down, nodded at the Negro, who took the telephone to set it on the floor near where it was plugged in.

'My God, Congressman,' groaned Koster, 'why didn't you let him phone?'

'Well, I feel I've been insulted enough for one night,' frowned Wade, 'I'm sure I have, and—'

'Gyaaaaah!' growled Trubel, throwing a hand tiredly at Wade. He opened and shut his mouth, then opened it to say, 'I got a friend down there, Congressman. Attorney-General's office. Call wouldn't have been traced.' He grunted and looked at Koster. 'See, Mr Koster? He won't be any problem. I could kill you right now, and tell him to go away.' He returned his eyes to Wade. 'Harmon Wade won't say a word to anyone.'

'Go on, go on,' Wade said, and coughed, himself, a small nervous cough. 'No one is paying attention to you, Mr Trubel. Go right on—make all the allegations you wish. It's your party. But we aren't listening.'

Trubel did not seem to be listening, himself. He patted Noreen's thigh softly, then glanced back at the projector and at Rexie My Riddle, frowning quizzically.

'Carson City,' said the Negro, who turned off the sofa lamp : quickly, again, there appeared the picture of the wistful child on the screen, with his gentle smile. It was there for several seconds, and then it was suddenly gone and in its place there was the picture of a young man talking to a policeman. In the darkness Cassius Koster rasped out :

'Oh my God—don't start that.'

Trubel's voice announced lowly : 'You guys were talking about that fellow, while back.'

'Terrence Philander Carol,' said the Negro from near the sofa. 'We don't know the name of the cop.'

Koster moaned, 'Leave me alone !'

'That picture,' said Lancelot Everybody, his voice abrupt because of its narrator-like impersonalness, 'was taken about thirty years ago, in Cambridge, Mass. The charley the fuzz's chatting with, he's President of Carol Pharmaceuticals of Providence and Passaic. At the time, however, he just stopped being a student, because of a little old scandal that involved Mr Koster and Mr Koster's sister Serena. Turns out the day before this picture was taken—'

'I already said I wouldn't say anything !' cried Koster in anguish in the darkness. 'Why don't you kill me, get it over with—why are you playing with me like this ! Stop it !'

The projector clicked, the image changed : the youth and the policeman were still there, but now they were fitted into the front page of an opened newspaper. The headline read : DEB SUICIDE, SOCIALITE SCANDAL.

The Negro read that headline aloud, and went on, 'Underneath, in case you can't read the subhead, that says: Brother Opposed Union. The brother in question was Mr Cassius Koster.'

The sound of something like scuffling followed the flash of a shadow across the room: Carson City Go at once had the overhead lights on. Koster was atop Trubel, a whimpering Noreen and grunting Trubel together fending him off—the Negro rushing over to yank Koster away forcibly, hurling him back to the sofa. Koster fell before the sofa on his knees, vented an outraged scream, clutched his heart under him and buried his face in the cushion of the sofa. Amsden was instantly leaning over him:

'Are you okay? Mr Koster!' Amsden took him by the shoulders, but Koster shoved him off, crying:

'Leave me alone! Why can't you leave me alone! This is hell, I'm dead and this is hell—*memory* is hell, why don't you let me forget!' He sobbed and Amsden tried to comfort him, clumsily, patting his back and encouraging him to sit up in the sofa.

At last Koster repossessed his self-control, pulled himself up to the sofa and huddled in its corner again, hiding his face.

'Mr Koster,' said Trubel, 'you're right. Memory is hell.' He snapped his fingers at Lancelot Everybody, nodding.

'About thirty years ago,' began the Negro—but Koster sat erect and forward, his face enraged, fists clenched, shouting:

'I'll tell it myself! Thirty years ago . . . thirty years ago Terry Carol was engaged to my sister. We were friends. He showed me one day copies of some exams he got hold of, well—they were worth his whole future, it seemed at the time. It was like he showed me a gold mine or something,' Koster's fists relaxed, he began to rub his hands together and stared wetly at the ceiling. 'He had millions. I couldn't—I was weak, I couldn't resist that kind of thing, I thought I could ask anything I wanted, so I . . . told him he had to make me his co-heir. I was crazy, crazy! I was just crazy. My father's business was in trouble then

and I didn't see it would pull out the way it did—there was the chance I'd leave school bankrupt. A chance like that, it wouldn't come again. So I wanted him to make this legal draft—privately—giving me co-ownership of Carol Pharmaceuticals on the death of his father, or else . . . I'd talk to the Dean of Studies. So—well, he got goody-goody, you know, all goody-goody, all shocked. He went to the Dean himself, the crumb. I mean hell, he could have talked me out of it, the goddam fool, but . . . he turned himself in and told the Dean what I'd said, so you know, we tried to keep it quiet. But the Dean was expelling both of us. There was no appeal. I mean Christ, there I was, not only about to be bankrupt but in complete disgrace, and my sister about to marry the bastard that caused it all. I mean, I told my sister how Terry finked on me, only . . . she took Terry's part. She said maybe Terry was only joking, but what I did was stinking, so. . . .'
Koster stopped and stared down at the hands he rubbed together, fell into a meditative silence and only when he suddenly grew aware of his hands and stopped rubbing them, folding them in his lap, did he glance up at Trubel, scowl down again and continue :

'I hated them both. This little sister I always took care of, we were close like—like twins, I guess. Practically twins. Instead of saying she'd never see *him* again, she said she wasn't going to see *me* again. Goddam, the whole thing was public, too, although the papers didn't take it up right away—but we knew they would and I used to dread going out for fear of what I'd find in some newspaper. I was really off my rocker; going crazy. My sister levelled off on me, she told me things I couldn't bear hearing, that's all. About how weak I was, how I wasn't a man, how she was going to marry him and forget she ever had a brother. I mean, this is the sister who when we were tiny, she could talk about marrying me some day —we were that close. That day, she got me so mad, so goddam mad, you know, I just kept telling her to shut up or I'd kill her, so she said, go ahead. Just made me so mad I nearly *did* kill her, I went for her to choke her, I was really strangling my own sister, I mean my whole head just turned off, stopped working. I saw those big tears of fright in her eyes all of a sudden, saw what I was doing, and first I felt so guilty, like waking up from some ugly nightmare in which I'd done every sin in the books—but then, feeling so sorry that way, her choking that way, I don't know, I burst into tears and went completely crazy—completely crazy, I—went crazy, started to love her instead of kill her, and . . . and I went crazy, that's all, I—my mind told me at least that would keep her from marrying Terry Carol, I. . . .' Koster all at once buried his face in his hands and began to sob into them, quiet, regular but back-racking sobs.

For some minutes, no one said anything. Koster's sobs and Trubel's wheezing were all that could be heard in the room. Finally, Trubel snapped his fingers and the Negro nodded.

'We ain't done,' said Lancelot Everybody. 'We got more pictures, Mr Koster.'

Koster said nothing. Gradually, he quieted his sobbing.

Amsden suddenly asked, 'Mr Trubel, can I pose a question?'

Louie Trubel sniffed a glance at Amsden.

Amsden chose to take the sniff and glance for permission, and asked, 'Doesn't Terrence Carol have a good deal more to do with this night than you've said so far? For example, I know his daughter. Congressman Wade has tussled with Carol's interests down in Washington. Don't you have some relationship with Carol?'

Trubel seemed to sneer at the question. He sighed at Amsden, as if he expected the question contained some simple avenue into its own answer, then snapped his fingers : the Negro bent, listened briefly, stood and, looking at Amsden, announced :

'Mr Trubel wants to say you're here tonight on the

charge of murder. There's no more to it than that. Mr Trubel's got no interest in Terrence Carol, he ain't got no connection with Terrence Carol. Mr Trubel wants to say people's lives are like what he calls a net. Like, if all the connections between all the lives in the world could be seen, everybody in the world would see he was connected with everybody else, and no one gets completely free of the net—not even by dying, because Mr Trubel says the net ain't just tossed over the face of the world. It gets thrown over time, too. Mr Trubel's idea is, people maybe instinctively know this, only they don't like to work their memories too hard, so they let themselves forget, only like they know it basically, see? Mr Trubel wants to say people get reminded of it sometimes, so maybe they get surprised to see how strangers meet and find out they got these connections; so they call it by the name "coincidence", like it's all a miracle or something. Like, you find out all of you got connections together, a connection called Terrence Carol, and it seems too freaky, so you think there's a plot with Terrence Carol in it. Only it ain't a coincidence, and it ain't a plot—it's just part of the net. Like, none of you figured you had this connection with Tommy Lincoln together, and you can see how that led to you all having connections with all of us and more people on each side. All this grooves on you like coincidence, only it's part of the net, and you probably got all kinds of connections you don't know about. Mr Trubel wants to say if you charleys ever stopped to think about the net a long time ago, maybe you'd've seen how you can't just act sloppy with your whole lives, because you got to think about even the connections you might have, if you're smart—because, man, one day you're going to discover they're real, they're really there, in life and death both. That's like Mr Trubel's outlook on life, right there. You got to watch your actions with your head, Professor, or you may get caught too tight in the net—see? Rexie, the slides ready?'

Carson City Go was at the lights again, and it was dark except for the screen, where—swiftly—the image of the newspaper vanished and its place was taken by a boy of twelve or thirteen in the portico of what appeared to be a church. Once again there was, though the face was small, a simple outward amiability, here combined with a wistfulness—the accretion of some maturity in the face suggested he had stopped questioning the miracle of the camera at last.

'That's Tommy at thirteen,' said the Negro. 'That was in his religious phase. He never got completely over his religion, although he could never quite figure out what his religion was—in his twenty years. Mr Trubel likes this picture, so we chose it, but the main point is, he was a kid, still cheerful, a human being, open to ideas. That was him. Okay, Rexie.'

Another click, and another image: a young man was graduating from high school. It was not a school photograph, but a parent's after-the-ceremony glance at his son, no longer a schoolboy. The outsizedly gleeful grin on the boy's face was somehow more the grin of the infant, seen in the first of the pictures: it was as if Tommy Lincoln was staring out at life, and life all at once looked like the mysterious camera and he was challenging it to explain itself. The Negro was saying:

'We could show you hundreds of shots between the ones we're seeing, here, only it'd just show you the same kid with the same ready grin. Maybe our point is just, he was a healthy kid, not always gloomy. Like, he was just Tommy, that's all. Okay, Rexie?'

Now the image was of a man in sports shirt and trousers and standing beside him, the youth, and Amsden was heard to grunt:

'Oh oh!'

The sober-faced man beside the solemn-faced youth was clearly Harry Amsden. There was, in fact, a cynical turn of the mouth on Amsden's face, somewhat imitated by a twist of the youth's mouth, but it might have been as easily called a sneer as a smile; and as if suspecting his mere expression might hang him, Amsden ventured :

'You caught me on an off day there, gentlemen. I don't remember that picture, by the way.'

Lancelot Everybody said, 'Tommy's friend, Drake, took that photo.'

'I don't remember Drake either,' said Amsden.

'Drake Meirdahl,' said the Negro.

'Meirdahl,' murmured Amsden. 'Yes . . . him I remember.'

'What do you make of those faces, Professor?' Trubel's voice rolled softly in the dark.

Amsden did not answer immediately, but finally said, 'I think you want me to say Tommy doesn't look as cheerful as he did when he was a baby.'

'This,' said the Negro, 'is one of five pictures we got with you in it, Professor. The expressions are only typical— like, the pictures we got from this entire period, with Tommy, they show the same thing : like he lost his—what do you call it, Professor? Wit? Optimism?'

'Illusions?' wondered Amsden.

'Rexie,' called the Negro, not taken enough with Amsden's lightheartedness to comment upon it.

'My God,' muttered Amsden, in amazement or simple disgust.

The image was a close-up of the two faces from the previous picture : two separate prints, side by side, the point in showing apparently being to emphasize either the sourness of mood or the patency with which the youth imitated the teacher. The intense narrow cast of the more demanding than inquiring eyes were the same. The mood they threw off was one of distrust.

'What'd you just eat?' asked the Negro. 'A lemon?'

'Face of a criminal, all right,' said Amsden.

'Yeah,' said the Negro, and paused briefly, then went on : 'Well, this is just background to pointing out how

Tommy forgot how to be cheerful once he started going to college. Not to pin nothing on you, Professor—but he sort of thought you knew the way around. One result was, he started to think it was us—his family—all messed up. I mean, like it had to be us or you.'

'So hang me,' muttered Amsden.

'He sure looks like you there,' said the Negro.

'Solar illusion,' said Amsden, refusing to desert his lightheartedness. 'Direction of the sun, Sir Lancelot. Two bodies caught in the same orbit on the same path, reflecting the same bleak social light.'

'Charley,' said the Negro sharply, wholly unamused, 'you ain't taught us nothing yet. We got a question for you, teacher: if you suddenly get grabbed by this idea that maybe everything in the whole damn world there is to know—all of it only makes life look dumb, pointless, like not worth breathing about—you know? Well, if you get that way, would you teach that to your students?'

'That's a very refined question,' said Amsden. 'It goes without saying a teacher has to teach what he believes.'

Carson City Go's face broke in still more lightheartedly than Amsden's tone, 'Nothing go without saying, Plofessor—not here!'

'All right,' muttered Amsden. 'I teach what I think. What else could I teach?'

'We were kind of figuring and hoping,' said the Negro, 'you might be able to make a case for the one thing a gangster can't always give his kid: like, how it pays off to have social responsibility.' He switched on the lamp and stood watching Amsden.

'Social *hypocrisy*, you mean,' retorted Amsden. 'That's what you wanted me to teach—hypocrisy!'

'*Yeah!*' Louie Trubel shouted, facing Amsden. His eyes burnt on Amsden and he took up his cane and squeezed it. '*Yeah!*' he shouted again. 'Hypocrisy! Like mine! I'm a gangster—okay. I think of myself as a businessman. I function that way. Listen—I do what I think is right. But

I'm human. I make mistakes, too. I'll tell you something : when I make bad mistakes—I put *myself* on trial, Professor. I'm human. You're human. Mr Koster, he's human. He makes mistakes. Now, if you want to keep the net from getting torn—listen, Professor : if you want to hold an organization together; hold society together, listen : you got to hold the best ideas way up high. High as you can. And be ready to face your mistakes. But don't advertise them. Don't fall in love with them. Don't pimp for them with children. Be a hypocrite! Shut up about it! You hear me, Professor Amsden? There's a difference : I ain't saying, be dishonest. Dishonesty stinks. But be human. Because I don't know history—but I know people. You don't never *get* a society where you don't need hypocrisy. The net's *made* out of hypocrisy—except like coincidence is a wrong word, and it's really the net—see?—hypocrisy's a lousy word, too. Agreement's a better word—yeah? You go against yourself. You pretend you're something if you ain't got the gut to believe in it—so *pretend,* at least! Where's your family that can function without hypocrisy? Where's your church or school or village can function without hypocrisy? I'll tell you : nowhere. You don't like hypocrisy? Tough! That's tough, Professor!' Trubel wheezed a while, his eyes still fire on Amsden, before he concluded just a bit more mildly, 'You don't have the guts to face what you got to be. You can't resist the girlies. You can't resist the kicks. So you figure to make your weakness right by passing it around, like some kind of New World communion wafer—yeah? Going to build a new society without hypocrisy—yeah? Professor,' Trubel began to cough, drawing out his handkerchief, 'you— you're,' he coughed into his handkerchief, wheezed a bit to catch his breath, then finished, 'you're a phony.' Suddenly Trubel leaned ahead, opening his mouth widely, Noreen bending over him, arm around him, her tone warmly anxious :

'Don't be excited, Louie honey, please, remember how

you vomit when you get too excited.'

Trubel opened and shut his mouth, looking as if he could not decide whether he was about to vomit just then or not. Finally he seemed to shudder, then slowly pushed his body back and wheezed a sigh up at Noreen. He muttered, 'I vomit.'

'Oh God,' murmured Congressman Wade then, shaking his head gloomily at Trubel. 'You're a fine one, Mr Trubel, to talk about holding up the best ideas. I fail—'

'Mr Trubel holds his ideas up,' the Negro interrupted to affirm. 'You call him gangster, Congressman. But he's an honest gangster. You don't like the sound of that? Tough! Mr Trubel wants to say an honest gangster's a better citizen than a dishonest politician. Say—we got a slide showing the totals of three bank accounts of yours. Shall I put them on?'

'*I'm* not going to defend hypocrisy,' scowled Wade. 'My money is legitimate. You people do what you want. I'm not going to say a word in my defence.'

'Good,' said Trubel, with a nod. 'Shut up.'

The Negro switched off the lamp, intensifying the youth and teacher upon the screen again; the picture sliding away to be replaced by the same youth as his face pulled away with exaggerated and possibly comical distrust from a girl beside him. The girl might merely have been trying to kiss his cheek. A soft moan from Koster seemed to identify the girl before the Negro could speak :

'This was taken just before Mr Trubel's son proposed to your well-behaved little girl, Mr Koster. It was pretty soon after the big seduction scene. Blow it up, Rexie.'

The boy's enlarged face was now pulling away over the shadow of his right shoulder. All aspect of what might have seemed a grin was alien to cheerfulness, the twisted mouth more nearly expressing revulsion while the eyes above were dulled beneath a melancholy turn of the brows.

Abruptly, that picture too was gone, a still larger blow-up appearing: the eyes, brows and forehead of the boy. The melancholy that had seemed dull now seethed in the huge eyes, some awful disappointment appearing to have settled in them. It looked not as if a pair of lips, but some threat to his very being might have faced such eyes.

'You'd think he already learned about your daughter, the way he looks, huh, Mr Koster?' asked Lancelot Everybody.

'I'm not even looking,' Koster said just above a whisper. 'My eyes are shut.'

'Oh, you better open them,' said the Negro. 'Why shouldn't you get your share of what your little girl passed around so freely?'

The image flashed away, replaced by one that instantly had Koster screaming out:

'Stop it!'

'Trina Koster gave,' began the Negro, but Koster screamed:

'Don't!'

The Negro sighed and seemed to wait to see if there would be any further interruptions to his narration of the photo on the screen, which might have been one of a group in packets sold by professional pornographers: girl and boy cheerfully espousing overt mutual affection for their garousedness together—except that unlike the professional pornographer's product, and with curious inappropriateness, these young people had even in their nakedness an extension of a higher rearing, a cleanness, a too-happy, too-self-willed forwardness, an awareness of what they were doing that put it outside of simple commerce. This youthful freshness of the two gave the picture greater power nearly like a beauty, but it also gave it a strange ugliness: one had the feeling the two had long before given up on the pleasures of hope, heart or head, and were helplessly seeking the barest common denominators together. Having given Koster some seconds to adjust to the image, the Negro at last proceeded:

'Trina Koster gave Tommy Lincoln a collection of shots like this. Only this one's notable, like, because she gave it to him just after rejecting his proposal of marriage. Like for a souvenir. That's not Tommy there—that's Drake Meirdahl. His father's a lawyer. You remember him now, Professor?'

Amsden muttered, 'Yeah.'

'We never found out who took the picture,' said the Negro, 'but it was over at Radcliffe. Maybe you recognize the room, Mr Koster. That was taken during visiting hours at her dorm, huh?'

All that was heard from Koster was a strange and frightening series of grunts, sharp inhalations, heavy gasps. Amsden cried :

'Turn on the lights !'

Carson City Go responded, and they all saw Koster alternately clutching at his shirt, leaning back, pounding at his chest, opening his mouth and rubbing his teeth together, squinting wildly up at the ceiling.

'You idiots !' Amsden cried. 'Look what you've done ! What the hell's wrong with you ! He told you he had a bad heart !'

Meanwhile, with Congressman Wade, who had rushed over to the sofa, Amsden worked to quiet Koster. Amsden was opening his shirt and he and Wade tried to lay Koster out along the sofa, but Koster shouted shrilly :

'Let me alone, let me alone !'

'Are you all right?' Amsden demanded with a quaking voice.

'Let me alone !' shouted Koster. 'Let me alone, let me die !'

'Don't you need a doctor?' asked Wade.

'Have you had an attack?' demanded Amsden. *Tell us!*'

'Let me alone !' shouted Koster, and he struggled free of them, swung his legs off the sofa, sat back and pounded his chest with a fury of self-hatred. 'No, goddam it !' he shouted and sobbed. 'I haven't had an attack, I'm *trying* to have an attack but it won't come! Oh God—why can't I die! What's wrong with me?'

'Quiet, now,' Wade tried to soothe him. 'Relax, Mr Koster.'

'Take it easy,' said Amsden, pulling Koster's pummelling fists away from his chest. 'For Christ's sake, Mr Koster, take it easy.'

'Why can't I get a heart attack *now*!' wailed Koster. 'Why do I have to wait till Dow-Jones goes down twenty points? Why can't I have an attack when I *want* one!'

As Koster quieted, Amsden turned on Rexie My Riddle and adopted the commanding voice that he might have used in some classrooms: 'You take that slide out of the projector before you turn off the lights!'

'Don't *you* defend me, Amsden!' snarled Koster. 'I don't need *your* defence! You *teach* that kind of thing!'

Amsden, stung by Koster's attack as he tried to defend the publisher, snapped waspishly back at him: 'Don't blame that on me! I never even heard of your daughter till tonight!'

'That boy was your student!' retorted Koster.

'Mr Koster,' Wade's tone implored, as he tried to get a word in.

'It's people like you who sell out other people!' Koster charged Amsden.

'What's wrong with nudity?' demanded Amsden. '*I* didn't publish *French for Adults*! You have faith in people right up to the time you find out your own daughter isn't acting according to your faith!'

'Professor,' said Wade, 'Mr Koster—'

'Are you trying to blame my daughter for that?' Koster snarled at Amsden.

'Girls deserve some freedom too,' said Amsden, 'wasn't that half of your philosophy?'

'Mr Koster,' Wade tried again in a strained and quickly impersonal tone, 'I didn't see that picture. I never saw it.'

Koster and Amsden had both risen to face each other,

and Wade tried to caution them both, a hand to the shoulder of each; but Amsden brushed Wade's hand away and turned on him :

'I thought you were taking a stand against hypocrisy !'

'This has nothing to do with hypocrisy !' answered Wade. 'I only—'

'*Hey*!' shouted Louie Trubel, suddenly. He glowered at the three of them and took his cane and rapped the floor. 'Sit down !'

Amsden glared at Trubel, then at Koster and then the glare wavered and he dropped his eyes. He sat at his end of the sofa and Koster, running his hands back over his thin hair, sat down shakily in his own place. Wade, shaking his head, retreated to his chair.

'We would have thought,' Lancelot Everybody said to Amsden once they all sat silently again, 'you'd have applauded our little show, here, Professor. I mean like, man, this is moral disobedience, ain't it? Ain't this like anarchy?'

'Even anarchy needs ordering,' said Amsden. Then he got his glare back and met Trubel's gaze directly. 'Anarchy doesn't mean disposing of simple manners. What you just did, the way you *use* stuff like that—you could *kill* someone !'

Trubel's cold, haughty eyes were unblinking in their confrontation with Amsden's heat. He said, 'It did,' and nodded before adding : 'It killed my son.' Then Trubel looked at the Negro, snapped his fingers.

The Negro said, 'Lights, Carson City.'

The lights overhead went out just as the projector clicked and the image on the screen was a portion of the United States Congress in session, focusing on a representative risen from his desk, mouth open.

'That's you, Congressman Wade,' said Lancelot Everybody. 'We got this shot from a friend of ours on a news magazine, and this one's from one of your filibusters against limiting the public's right to get hold of guns. There are *some* gangsters running around who were really on your side, there, Congressman. Hey, Rexie—what was it you said when you saw this shot of our defiant representative?'

From his station by the projector, Rexie My Riddle's voice grinned gravelishly: 'Would you put a gun in this man's hand?'

'Hey, we got another picture of the Congressman,' said the Negro. 'Rexie?'

On the screen, now, was a softer image of Wade's expressible features, perhaps reminiscent of the more retrospective picture of Trubel's son: the eyes thinly speculative, a small turn of the mouth suggesting a mild bemusement, the half-shut eyes giving the face an inwards-looking aspect.

'Remember that shot, Congressman?' It was Trubel's voice low across the room, and dark as the room's corners.

Wade was hesitant, then said, 'No—I do not.'

'We better put it in context, man,' said Lancelot Everybody. 'Rexie!'

The image went to be replaced by another picture: the face was seen to be leaning from a window, outwards, hands gripping the sill, and the eyes that had been half shut and inwards-looking in the larger perspective were seen to be downwards-looking. The bemusement was still there.

'It ain't always so easy,' said the Negro, 'to get hold of a shot of Congressman Harmon Wade looking so pleased with the world, but we managed to come up with that one. Rexie, let's see what was entertaining Congressman Wade, there.'

Quickly the image was changed: a body twisted in a street, flames leaping from all its parts except the face alone. The shirt, trousers, the hair, the shoes, they were all hidden in flame. The fist-clenching hands and the face alone seemed to rise from the flames, both lifted supplicatingly. It could not be certain whether the eyes were open or shut. The widely opened mouth gave the face an aspect of shock more than of pain. Flames removed, it might have been the face of a completely beaten prize-fighter a split second after the impact of a knockout blow.

'Meanwhile,' the Negro narrated, 'high on the seventh floor Congressman Harmon Wade turned to his secretary and said, "And me without a single marshmallow".'

'I said *no* such thing!' cried Wade. 'I *know* how that got reported, and I fired the girl who let such an idea get publicized. I said *no* such thing!'

'Maybe not,' said the Negro. 'Rexie?'

A blow-up from out of the fire brought the face from the flaming aureole, a mystifyingly religious fervour in the face that no longer bore any trace of what might be called shock or even surprise. The eyes seemed just partly open, though probably blind, and the smouldering retinas might have been so tense as to make the fallen lids as tautly constricted as they seemed : as if the flames were strangling him from within. The mouth was seen now to be so misshapen in its contortions that only the fire's core-searing pain could have concocted such a crookedly twisted stretch of lips. The very skin of the face seemed bloated. It was a face that did not merely suffer, however : it contained some mystery—as if it were halfway into the discovery of death, as if by the light of the fire within the boy had 'seen' : such a face, had it been painted, might have been praying, apart only from the broken line of the mouth.

No one spoke.

Without instructions, Rexie My Riddle—either having been previously instructed, or simply inspired—reset the projector to show the first blow-up of Congressman Wade, the mild bemusement which now seemed, in contrast, a too vapid, a too settled expression, which was therefore as profanely unacceptable as might have been a happy grin : it seemed, indeed, a grin in contrast. The Riddle reproduced the blow-up of the boy in agony—then began to flick the two slides back and forth, slowly, one and the other, then more quickly, the suffering boy : the bemused congress-

man : the performer : the audience : the boy : the
congressman : the caring death : the uncaring life : the
mysterious flame : the empty desert : the warring youth :
the ruling age : Tommy Lincoln : Harmon Wade, until
Noreen all at once cried :

'Oh, Rexie, stop it, please ! It isn't religious !'

Carson City Go snapped on the overhead lights, washing
the room in cold electric incandescence.

Trubel, expressionless, sat gazing off at nothing. He
lifted a hand to pat Noreen's thigh, as she sniffled behind
the hand she held over her face.

Lancelot Everybody, standing near Trubel's chair once
more, reshifted himself, coughed into one hand, rubbed
his hands lightly together and looked very much the
master-of-ceremonies resuming charge of nothing more
serious than a variety show. He gave his nose a rub and
finally said :

'We could go on, charleys—only, like we don't have to
take all night about it. Details, like stats of the Congressman's bank statements or more pictures from *Playboy* or
windy chitchat about how Professor Amsden thinks the
world should stop turning until he's ready to turn with it
again—maybe it ain't all that interesting. The point is,
Mr Trubel wants you to remember how careful he was. He
took his time. He spent plenty. He wanted to be sure. He
made himself doubt himself, he even made himself doubt
his son. Only, no matter how many times we went over it,
we never could stop doubting you people, either—groove?
So there you are, charleys . . . how do you plead?'

Wade was prompt to reply. 'Not guilty, of course,' he
said. 'But you know as well as we do there's no chance of
you accepting that plea.'

'Go ahead, man,' the Negro threw a hand out. 'Plead.'
Amsden said, 'You left out a suspect, Sir Lancelot.'
'Yeah?' said the Negro.

'You left one out,' nodded Amsden. 'Louie Trubel.'

'Goddam it,' hissed Koster, 'take it easy!'

'Why the hell?' scowled Amsden. 'The deck's stacked.'

Koster went on in the same hiss, as if he thought only Amsden might hear him, 'Do you have to make them even *madder*?'

'For Christ's sake,' Amsden squealed in frustration. 'It was just a couple minutes ago they were showing—'

'Never mind a couple minutes ago,' Koster interrupted, his hiss rising to meet the pitch of Amsden's squeal. He glanced at Trubel, back at Amsden. 'Look,' he forced his eyes back to Trubel. 'Look—I'm sorry I tried to jump you. Yes—and I'm sorry for what happened to my daughter and your son.'

'What happened to your daughter?' asked Louie Trubel. 'Huh, Mr Koster?'

'I don't know! The times, the goddam madness of the goddam times, the . . . I sure as hell never thought a thing like this could happen. I would *never* have let her have the goddam pill if I thought she could get so confused, so goddam *dumb*, to let herself get pulled around that way. I *don't* believe in that. Mr Trubel, I know she's good at heart, my little girl is—I *know* that. I know my little girl.'

Trubel stared at Koster.

Koster stared back, his eyes his plea of defence.

The Negro asked Koster, 'You gave your daughter the pill?'

'Well, I mean,' blinked Koster, '. . . I gave her permission to request them of our family doctor. Sure. If she absolutely *needed* them. I mean, my God—*I* know what happens in colleges these days. I didn't want her getting pregnant.'

'Did you give her some aspirins too?' asked Amsden.

'Shut up!' snapped Koster.

Trubel shook his head, waved a hand at the Negro and at Amsden. 'Mr Koster—you told her she could have them?'

Koster went red in the face again, and a scowl twisted his brow. 'You're damned right I did! And I'm glad I did! You don't think I wanted her coming home some day with yours or anyone else's grandchild in her belly, do you?'

'Yeah,' muttered Trubel. His lips twitched for a few moments and he sniffed. 'You didn't want that.'

'*Every* father knows things happen these days, and unless he's a complete moron, he does what he can to prevent a baby from crawling in between families. Look— I didn't think she'd let it happen. But I knew it *could* happen—that's the thing. I mean, my God, Mr Trubel, girls are human too. If boys're going to run around with a hundred and fifty per cent freedom, why shouldn't girls have *some* freedom!'

Louie Trubel asked, 'What freedom?'

'*No* special freedom!' groaned Koster, looking as if he was sorry he had allowed himself to get tangled in the debate. 'Goddam it, I'm not trying to antagonize you. I'm just saying, if boys are supposed to be out for a good time, why not girls?'

Trubel's empty old face stayed on Koster's like a shadow. 'Mr Koster, I never taught my boy that. To go out and have a good time. Why did you teach your girl that?'

'I didn't say I taught her that!'

'What did you teach her?'

'I taught her she's human—and that's all I taught her. I taught her to mind her dignity, and not let boys push her around—that's what I taught her. I taught her to be honest and never pretend she's anything but what she is, and if she *does* get messed up, to come and tell her father right away. And if she got into some situation where she couldn't do that and couldn't hold the line—just be sure she had a line of pills behind her, at least. I taught her to be a free, equal, independent human being, and to respect herself.'

Trubel nodded. He took up his cane and fingered it, studying it morosely for a time. Then he looked at Koster again. 'Did you ever teach her to respect other people, Mr Koster?'

'Naturally,' scowled Koster. 'But it's no use respecting others if you don't respect yourself. I taught her to be a woman!'

'Wait, wait,' muttered Trubel, waving his cane at Koster. He shook his head. 'No, Mr Koster.' He opened and shut his mouth, then looked irritably at the Negro, as if he had failed to find the words he wanted.

'No,' said the Negro. 'You didn't teach her to be a woman, Mr Koster. You taught your daughter to be a cunt. You taught her to pass herself around, like you got the idea that was some kind of equality. Only Mr Trubel, he's a Sicilian, an old-fashioned Sicilian, so he don't understand men who pass their women around. Never mind it's a father or husband or lover, someone passes his woman around—I'll tell you, charley : we know we got a funny breed of man, there, who ain't like a man. Wasn't that what your sister said, charley?'

'You son of a bitch!' Koster growled at Lancelot Everybody, fists clenched on his knees. His eyes slashed at Trubel. 'What do I care if you're a Sicilian! This is America!'

Trubel nodded and touched his cane to his chin. 'You permanent residents,' he said, 'you don't value your women any more?'

'We value them plenty!' cried Koster. 'Enough to want them to be able to live as freely as men.'

'Mr Koster,' said Trubel, 'I'm going to tell you something. You got no loyalty.'

'Loyalty!' Koster spat the word out as if it tasted foul. 'Your idea of loyalty, Christ's sake—it smells of ghosts, it's old, it's old as, as—'

'As what?' asked the Negro. 'Time? Religion? Love? The net? Old as what?'

130

'As old, old,' Koster stammered on in his furious anguish, 'it's old as *death*!' Distrusting his own simile, he immediately winced.

Rexie My Riddle asked from the table where the projector stood, 'As old as whose death, Mr Koster? As old as Tommy Lincoln's death?'

'Death still vely much in fashion, Mr Koster,' smiled Carson City Go, perkily. 'Still vely new!'

Louie Trubel sighed and sat back, then nodded ponderously at the Negro. 'Lanny,' he muttered. 'Letter.'

Lancelot Everybody nodded, lifted a finger to secure a moment's delay and went to the table to pour himself a small ration of whisky. He slipped that down his throat quickly, set the glass down and, meandering back to Trubel's side, drew from his pocket a large white envelope. From the envelope he withdrew several sheets of paper and unfolded them.

'Item,' he said. 'One letter.' He waved it at the Chinese.

'I identify!' smiled the Chinese. 'I know that letter. Tommy lite that letter, leave in motel loom inside his gleen laincoat. I wake up, see coat, no Tommy, I think : him not go so far, leave coat this way. Go back to sleep. Much too late I find letter. Yes, that the letter.'

'This letter is submitted as evidence, charleys,' said the Negro. 'It was addressed to Mr Trubel and Noreen.'

'Wait,' said Trubel, lifting a hand to the Negro. 'Say— let Noreen read the letter.'

'Oh shit,' murmured Noreen nervously, only grudgingly receiving the envelope and sheets of paper from the Negro. 'Out loud?'

Trubel coughed and sniffed and settled himself, as Noreen unfolded the sheets gingerly and unhappily, then stared down at the first page as if uncertain of her ability to read the boy's hand.

Soon, 'Dear Papa, Dear Noreen,' she began, but faltered over, 'I'm going to be,' her voice dropping away. She looked at Lancelot Everybody, but he made no offer to take the letter back, so she cleared her throat, rose from the arm of the chair, choosing to stand as she read, and began again:

'Dear Papa, Dear Noreen,
'I'm going to be dead when I'm twenty, and on my twentieth birthday maybe you'll look at this letter again and try to figure out why I'm dead.

'Papa, you and Noreen tried so hard for me. Maybe you even tried too hard—like you tried to give me things to believe in and live for, so that sort of made me into someone who *needed* something to live for, just to live. But I'm grateful for that, because to be that way is the thing that made life worth living all the time I've lived it—and death is dearer to me, with that, than a moment's breath without it.

'And yet I'm ashamed of my actions, now. I'm ashamed of my life. I guess I inherited too much old-fashionedness from you, and find I cannot live up to my century. I tried to, and I tried to pretend I was right to do what I did, like when I wrote you to disown you and Noreen. What a jerk I was, like to use a word, *disown,* maybe I could rewrite truth by the scratch a pen makes on paper. Only, now you're going to think I'm *really* disowning you, because I'm taking from you all I ever owned that I could give you. I mean myself.

'Papa, I wish I could give myself back to you. I wish I could put out of my head a thousand things that took up housekeeping in there. But I can't. Remember you taught me never to let any girl into my soul I didn't want to live with the whole rest of my life? I know what you meant, but the thing is, I did let this girl in, and she's still there and will never leave me. (I know that too—you were right.) But it's not just her down there having this funeral party in my soul, it's just a thousand things, all sharp and cutting, that tore so many holes in my soul all the innocence just dripped out, slowly, helplessly, stupidly, painfully. And the ugly things formed scabs there, and my memory keeps picking at the hideous scabs to let them bleed again, and again, and again, and the sores are there forever.

'I've lost my faith, like I told you, Papa. But it's like— I think maybe like a girl who just forgetfully slides off her virginity, if you see. I mean, I value it more now that I've lost it, but it can't come back. I have a scab where I used to keep my prayers.

'I lost my trust of love, and that's like losing another kind of faith, just as deep. I want love all the more because it has fled forever. Love festers on my soul like pain, and there's no way I can love except to hurt, ever again. I don't even want to. I don't even want to.

'I lost my belief in goodness—not *my* goodness, because I still believe in the existence of selfishness. But when you *know* things, where can you put knowledge so it stops hurting—like, I know everything I once thought of as hopefulness and meaningfulness are only egotistical wishes I had for myself. Childishly. I can see this. What right have I to solicit "meanings" for my life, when my very concept of "nobility" is only going to damage others (and how can one have "nobility" in one's own name?). Nobility is dead. Like Norman Mailer (he's a novelist) wrote the word "noble" is silly except as an adjective to modify four-letter words. You see what I mean? I could maybe move my bowels in front of the White House or something, and that would be "noble", whatever that word means now—oh Papa, the whole thing is, I don't know what words *mean* any more. The century you taught me, and this century—all the meanings are different. So I can't even have the freedom of acting "good", because I know my "goodness" is only a selfish thing. But that's not the hurt of it : the thing I can't stand is losing my faith in the goodness of *others*. I can't stand *knowing* or even having to care about ego and self-interest and—I mean, I want to believe, and if I can't, that robs me and my existence of any real meaningfulness.

'The girl I love, though (yes Papa! I still love her, because I can't love again anyhow, and she's what's in my soul, and whatever that love was is the love I've got, till this morning burn it out of me)—but she told me something the opposite of what you used to teach me (and I'm sorry Papa, but for this century I guess she's right and you're wrong) : she must respect herself first, before she can really respect others, or free herself before she can care about the freedom of others, or understand herself in order to understand others. My father taught me I have to respect others before I can respect myself, and understand myself through others. (Papa, I said she's right—but it's your way I understand and love, which makes me feel close to you right now, even if it hurts too much to stay alive when I can't even have any real insights into my own *Age*!) Professor Amsden pointed out once how Bertrand Russell (he's a philosopher) said "Love thyself above thy neighbour", so you see, my girl wasn't alone in thinking that way in her time. And the meaning *is* good : it just means, if you don't love and respect yourself first, how can you love and respect others? I believe I understand this, intellectually—*but I can't make myself live that way!* I can't *do* it! Every time I really do put my own interests first, every time I say, "Okay—Tommy first, then women and children, then everyone else", I don't know, it's like a whole sea of horror flows over me, an instinctual sea echoes mocking laughter at me saying *Wrong! Wrong! Wrong!* It's like I can't learn because I'm too full of the other century, or the past, and I feel guilty in even trying to honestly search out the righteousness in private pleasure for the sake of public destruction. Papa, my soul frightens me.

'I don't know why it all means so much to me. I must be too different from others. I'm an anachronism, devoid of the principles and hopes of my very generation. But

134

then, it hardly matters in a way, because I'm just a stupid soulful of sores, anyhow. How horrible it is to realize, abruptly, you aren't one of those who can measure up to the beautiful, tough ideal called Truth. That takes a special bravery, maybe.

'I'm not at all brave, in what I am about to do. (Brave! I just wish my Chinese uncle sleeping near me here, would wake up and pound some sense into me, knock off the scabs, cauterize my soul and drag me home to you, Papa, and to Noreen—the two best people in the whole world, including *everyone* in the world, heroes and philosophers and teachers, including Professor Amsden, whose idealism I wish I could live up to, and hope in terror I am "dying" up to this morning.) No, I just won't pretend I've got bravery. If I had that, I'd stay alive, get tough, hurl myself at Truth, conquer my dumb old-fashioned timidity. And wouldn't be so scared just now, when all my recent thoughts have been about death itself.

'The way I choose to die is terrible to me. If I was still religious, I couldn't even do it (any more than, if I was still religious, I could die without the Sacrament: forgive me for that, but it would be a false Sacrament even if it were available to me). The method of this death somehow seems to me to have been appointed by those who still *are* religious, but not of a religion I could ever understand. I am emulating Buddhists, in my dying, who found in flames a purification and commiseration with their people, sacrificed daily in the flames of war. I have not got a natural fire, like Professor Amsden, that can burn indignantly with a personal responsibility for things that happen in his name. It is obvious he is right to struggle against ugly and immoral acts, and to destroy, therefore— but unlike him, I am unable to live with that responsibility. Therefore, I have decided to die in support of it.

'I must die for something. It is the one Beauty I linger beside, that makes my closing breath sweet to me: to die for something is to have lived for something. Scabrous and faithless as I am, still I will not bear just throwing my life away. I want it to be at least a symbol of meaningfulness, the meaning so clear it would serve for any century, yours or Professor Amsden's or my girl-friend's or even my own (whatever century *that* is!).

'You will learn I have died before where Congressman Wade has his office. I am choosing an hour when I know he will be there. Once, Papa, I would not have said I really hate, hate personally, a human being; but I guess I do hate Wade. He is like something purely evil to me. I wish I could burn him with me. Noreen will shudder to read that, but I am just being honest about my feelings. Maybe it's all in the century again, and so way past my understanding, but I don't see how it is millions of people can calmly get serious about Wade's idea to just napalm and defoliate and maybe atom-bomb a country away, on the grounds that way over there, they are "aggressive". Then I remember how he tried to humiliate you in Washington, Papa, and you could laugh it off, but I could not so easily, because I knew you were a better man than him. Then I remember how, in this book about President Kennedy's assassination, the first thing Wade thought about afterwards was defending Texas, and the next thing defending guns. In a way, I feel a gladness he is your enemy as well as mine. It adds to the sense of meaning I am trying to feel about my death. At the same time, I know I am only conditionally "right", because millions of people can't be wrong and only me "right", and besides I feel this awful hatred of the man oozing like pus, poisonous and thick and deep, from the wounded pores of my soul. So I know I am being emotional. Somewhere inside the emotion, though, there is a sense of "rightness", and that is holding me up right now. I cherish that. It is my Beauty.

'Papa, I have a last wish to ask of you. It will hurt, but please do it for me. Do not claim my body. Let a friend, outside the business, claim my body and see to the burial.

Then please visit my grave. I ask this for many reasons, and here are a few. I don't want my death on your shoulders. That is important to me. Some people will say I died because of being your son, and will try to make out the gesture had no meaning and so I didn't even believe in what I did. This would hurt you, and hurt Noreen, and hurt me in my death. Please don't let my dying be robbed of its living meaning. I told my girl-friend I was your son, and she half believed and half did not, and was not nice about it anyhow. But when someone else collects my body, with the name Lincoln (I know you are a genius and can manage that), then she will just think I was lying for some reason. That's okay. Let her. I don't care what she thinks about anything. But please abide by this one wish of mine, as it contains the meaning of my life.

' "The meaning of my life", as I write those words, makes me remember the last paragraph from a book I talked to you about once (did you read it?). It was by Leonard Hanna, *The Deaths of Others,* the book about the first decade of the Community Experiment Hanna is conducting in Turkey—incidentally, my girl-friend's father published that book. I used to have the whole last chapter learned by heart, back when I was just ready to go to Kingston, because I valued the ideas and thought to learn from them. Only now, I can hardly remember anything at all except the very last paragraph. I used to have a clear idea about what I thought it meant, but now I'm less sure. Maybe, though, it will have some meaning for you, right now. In any event, Papa, it occurs to me to write it down :

' "The meaning of life and the meaning of death are inextricably united in a common weave"—isn't that like your "net", Papa?—"nor can life be meaningful when death cannot be. Therefore, any belief which holds life to be the whole meaning of existence, and which despises or fears or simply disregards death, might best be regarded as a temporary belief, that cannot endure : this is true simply because death is true—and therefore, death must be acceptable. In this sense, they are not the ideas which raise death to life's stature of significance which should be likened to either an opiate or mere escapism; but rather, the ideas which belittle death, or attempt to circumvent its genuine importance, force a cynical, often hedonistic, escapism upon all the accoutrements of life. There is, as has been described, reason to suppose a belief which in some simple form of ritual honours the dead (indeed, may accord to the individual dead within an intimate circle, particularly the family, a permanent 'presence' or 'living spirituality') is at once the least strain on human reason (in that death must remain essentially the great Mystery) and the most directly satisfying article of faith to which the human individual may respond, to give life richness, to give death meaning. Surely, at all events, there is no way to separate a real value of the life of any individual—including oneself—from the deaths of others."

'Please, Papa, if you understand that, then receive solace by honouring me in death—even if, in life, I have failed to honour you. Let me live at home—because if a spirit *does* exist in me, Papa, Noreen, it will never want to leave you. You will feel it sometimes when things are quiet there, and you meditate with your souls. I will always be in your house. In my room.

'I love you all, all my big family, as best a bewildered, self-betrayed and unwhole soul can love at all. And shall love you better, once again with purity, after the fire.

'Your grateful son,' Noreen concluded almost emptily, tonelessly, giving no expression to the name, 'Tommy.'

She slowly folded the papers over, and looked at no one as she resumed her seat on the arm of Louie Trubel's chair.

Trubel glowered at her. 'Did he write "shit" once?'

'Don't, Louie,' murmured Noreen, frowning. 'He wasn't perfect. He was human.'

Amsden had silently opened the book he held to its final page. He had felt a quickening, nearly a stinging, of intellect as Noreen read the reference to the very book he had withdrawn from the bookshelves. He knew it was only coincidence, but it felt more like Trubel's net in the way it personalized the letter—as if somehow it had been directed peculiarly to him as much as to the boy's father. He felt another quickening of his senses as the reference to this room was read, and Amsden had glanced off at the cupboard, as if expecting to see Tommy Lincoln standing there, with his books.

Congressman Wade was the first to speak: 'It was a very moving letter, Mrs Trubelli. Even with his passion of hatred for me, his passion is touching in that letter. I expect there is no soul that is not wounded here on earth —my own has been wounded many times. Most recently, just a few minutes ago, as you read of that boy's hatred for me. I speak the truth, Mrs Trubelli. But my philosophy tells me to go on living with my wounds, and to continue as best I can to overcome my weaknesses and do the best I can for my family and my state.'

Amsden, closing the book in his lap, shook his head and drew out a cigarette. 'The more you think about it, the more lost you get.'

Trubel turned to Amsden.

'All this concentration on your son's death,' Amsden said softly, smoke spewing from his mouth. He blew out the match, dropped it in the ashtray. 'The more you think about it, the more intricate it becomes. It's like your net: one idea comes from another, joins another, melts into another. I mean, you just want to blame one of us for what happened. But you can't—not rationally, Mr Trubel.'

Trubel nodded. Then he asked, 'Who should I blame?'

'I haven't the vaguest,' said Amsden. 'Maybe no one. But I didn't invent the words I use and I didn't invent the tenor of the times. Your son's respect for my ideas—I mean, we liked each other, but *that* degree of respect—it baffles me. I try to inspire, of course, but I've never pretended I have a grain of real leadership in myself. And then, if it's the sexual mood of the times you want to hold responsible—I mean, even if you restrict your outrage to college campuses—well, you have to blame just about everyone you see on nearly any campus. Look, Mr Trubel : students know what they want before they ever get to college, these days. And if they aren't quite sure, there are plenty of students already on campus to tell them. There are political groups and arty groups and freedom groups and *all* kinds of groups. The kids pretend they've done away with fraternities and sororities, they want to think they're independent now, but they just join other, and often larger, groups. They have to be hip, or militants, or heads, or reactionaries. They have to groove on the same ideas, the same songs—look, it even includes officials of your local university. If you run out of pot some night and you can't wait, just call your local Dean or college President. And if it's vengeance you want, you're going to have to put deans and presidents and vast armies of people, younger and older, on trial here. The kids have *won*, Mr Trubel. That's what I learned, and that's what you're fighting. I mean, if you want to collect every college official, every dean and president, who lets girls in boys' rooms and boys in girls' rooms full well knowing what's happening, and who knows damned well he'll never catch up with all the drugs around so he sits back and lights up, instead—well, Mr Trubel, you're going to need to turn your whole farm, here, into a courtroom, and it'll be damned crowded. And that's just talking about merry old Academe. What about all the fathers or, for that matter, doctors of Mr Koster's persuasion—you think *he* made his philosophy, all by himself? You think Wade started the war or personally created the United States Congress in his own image? You honour us too highly, Mr Trubel: you credit us with a lot more power than any one of us can have, individually. But it doesn't stop there. Because, when you try to place the blame on Koster, for example, you're really blaming something far beyond intent or even awareness; so you have to find everyone in that net of yours whose mistakes lean into Koster's. And as you know, that's a kind of limitless leaning. What it all adds up to, Mr Trubel, is that you'll have to use your whole farm and spend the rest of your life at hearings, if you want to make even a start at pinning down responsibility for the death of Tommy Lincoln. And you'll never be done with the job.' Amsden puffed irritably on his cigarette, nearly burnt out, and dashed it into the ashtray. 'Never! But set all that aside, and you still have a big hole in your prosecution. You left out the professionals, the criminals who aren't criminals by interpretation only. Gangsters, Mr Trubel—just like you. You *are* responsible, and your son himself said, in his letter, you helped make him what he was: you built him into an anachronism. And that wasn't all you did. You lived your life way outside the beaten civil path, exactly as I did. How did I isolate Tommy Lincoln any more than *you* isolated him? If he couldn't face the world as it was, wasn't it because his father made it impossible for him to face the world? I mean hell, Mr Trubel—there was a boy who had to lie about who he was, only to have some peace in college!' Amsden quickly lighted another cigarette.

Trubel's eyes had been solemn and nearly blinkless upon Amsden during the long challenge, and he kept watching Amsden even after the speech had ended. 'Professor,' he said, 'this is only a simple court.' He sighed wheezily, snapped his fingers at the Negro.

'Mr Trubel wants to say,' Lancelot Everybody carried on, 'like this is only a simple court, and if the net gets torn, you got to find some justice. You got to discriminate

—like, maybe your ideas ain't even yours, Professor. But you're the charley that pushed them. Maybe Mr Koster's mistakes ain't unusual. But in the death of Tommy Lincoln, the mistakes were Mr Koster's—not someone else's. Maybe, like, everyone down in Washington ain't any more dependable than the yellow rose of Texas, here—only, man, he was the one that took the trouble to give Mr Trubel's son a bed of cause to die in; groove? You got to discriminate, Professor. That's what any kind of law or system is. That's where the hypocrisy comes in and you can't shove it out. You got to discriminate.'

'Racially?' muttered Amsden.

'But your son,' interjected Harmon Wade loudly, 'he'd only have found something else to die for. You read the letter—he *wanted* to die!'

'Mr Trubel's son found you,' said the Negro. 'Mr Trubel wants to say Tommy Lincoln's gesture worked, Congressman. Maybe, in your mind, something else made people start thinking less and less of the Four Bombs Proposal. Only Mr Trubel wants to remind you, Congressman, back then on the day his son stopped in front of your office, you were a real popular cat—real popular. You had people scared, Mr Congressman. Like, there was a time when Mr Trubel thought a charley like you could make sense, himself. Yeah—you really had people to the point of thinking only some kind of agent for the Viet Cong would even stand against you. But after Tommy Lincoln's death, there were those big, silent death marches outside your window, every week for nearly a half year. Fuzz'd chase them away, but man, they'd only come back. Tear gas didn't stop them. They carried two kinds of signs only, if you don't remember. One was *No Bombs*. The other was: *Tommy Lincoln*. Like maybe the mood and times changed, maybe Tommy Lincoln had nothing to do with it. But man, all at once no one was shivering in front of Harmon Wade no more. We followed all that real close, charley—you just betcha. We got very moved by all that, and used to go to Tommy's grave to tell him what was happening. That was real good.'

'Well, Mr, uh . . . Everybody,' mumbled Wade, 'if you think that boy's act in any way influenced the assessment of those who had to vote on my proposal, then your understanding of the way this country works is very—'

'Gyaaa*aaah*!' growled Trubel, and waved Wade's words away, turning his contorted face off so that he need not look at the congressman. He found himself gazing back at the bookshelves and presently he nodded a bit. 'Them books—I read them. All of them.' He stared at them so hard it seemed he was attempting to see his son through the texts in literature, politics, history, philosophy. He closed his eyes abruptly and heaved his large old head around, muttering, 'Defence.'

The Negro slipped his hands into his pockets and looked at the suspects again. 'There's no charge on you charleys now. Your tongues got open season. Anything you want to say to defend yourselves this is the time. Congressman?'

Wade at once sat forward, elbows on thighs, glaring at Trubel. 'I won't offer a defence, Mr Trubel—only a warning : whatever you do, it cannot be kept hidden. You are wrong to think I am afraid of you. But even if I did honour a silence in deference to your shock and sorrow, you could not maintain a secret as awful and barbaric as this indefinitely. Maybe you read somewhere in your son's books, over there, an old saying from the classics : murder will out.'

Trubel nodded and mumbled. 'Yeah. I did.'

'Is that all?' the Negro asked Wade.

Wade blinked, his glare faded and he sat back dejectedly. 'That's all,' he whispered.

The Negro turned on Koster. 'Got a statement, charley?'

Koster looked unprepared and as agonized as if he had been condemned already. 'My family,' he suddenly invoked, voice quivering. 'Look, I'm scared for my family. They aren't going to understand, they *need* me, Mr

Trubel! And after all that's been said just tonight, my
God—I can't leave my little honey without understanding.
I got to try and *help* her! Look ... look: let us go—let us
all go. There must be some other way to satisfy you than
taking a life!'

Trubel shook his head sombrely.

'Professor Amsden?' asked the Negro.

Amsden gazed evenly at Louie Trubel. 'Well—I've still
heard no prosecution and no defence for the fourth suspect.'
He hardened his eyes on the old man.

Trubel nodded and nearly managed a smirk. 'I hear
you, Professor,' he said. He sat contemplating privately,
lips moving, pushing out and pulling in his wheezy breath.
He finally said, 'No—no, Professor. I'm going to satisfy
you.' He sniffed at the Negro. 'Lanny, listen. We got four
suspects. Louie Trubel accuses Louie Trubel of the murder
of Tommy Lincoln—his son.'

'No!' cried Noreen instantly. 'I won't let you do that,
Louie!'

'Listen, Noreen,' murmured Trubel without looking up
at her. 'I do that. Because I don't know.'

Carson City Go piped unhappily, 'You not do wise thing,
Mr Tlubel!'

'If you do that,' Noreen said anxiously, 'I'm a suspect,
too. I accuse myself!'

'Hey, shut up,' muttered Trubel. 'I don't want that. I
accuse myself. I'm a gangster. I taught him too, like
Professor Amsden says. I took chances. Amsden's right: I
made him lie. Okay. I accuse myself.'

Amsden peered around at his fellow suspects with a
quick intensity, his eyes pausing on Koster before he asked,
'Who's on the jury?'

'I was on the jury,' said Trubel. 'Now I'm off. The
jury is Noreen, Lanny, Carson City and Rexie. They'll
vote.

'Oh yeah—thanks,' Koster nodded, wretched and sar-
castic, 'that's great. I'm overcome with your generosity.

Look, let *us* vote. Let's all vote, and see if you have the guts to execute yourself if *you* lose, Mr Trubel!'

Trubel faced Koster, his lips quivering and pouting. He said, 'I wouldn't lose.'

'A secret vote,' suggested Wade, his voice not quite even. 'If we had a secret vote, it would be fair. Otherwise, it isn't fair.'

Trubel snorted and nodded at Wade. 'Congressman—you think I'm dumb?'

Wade hung his head a little and said softly, 'No, not dumb. Just a coward.'

'Listen,' said Trubel. 'Suspects don't vote. Including me.'

'It's easy to call yourself a suspect,' said Amsden, 'when you've got only your friends on the jury, when you don't hear any prosecution against yourself, and when the only people who might think *you're* responsible for Tommy Lincoln's death aren't allowed to think, much less vote. Why shouldn't we get a year to prepare a case against *you*?'

'Listen!' roared Trubel, and taking up his cane he gave the floor a cracking rap. His mouth waggled for a while before he could make himself say : '*You're* on trial here—not me!'

'Then you lied,' snapped Koster. 'You don't really accuse yourself at all.'

Trubel huffed madly and shook his head and finally muttered, eyes up on the Negro, 'All three of my suspects, they turn out shyster lawyers. They get together to pin it on me.' He scowled at Koster. 'Say—didn't you hear Tommy's letter?'

'You're goddam right I did,' Koster returned scowl for scowl. 'Sounded like he felt you didn't toughen him up for the world. Sounded to me like he didn't have anything at all to blame on Professor Amsden, for example. Sounded to me like he went right on being in love with my daughter. Maybe that says something for her, Mr Trubel.'

'You're afraid,' said Amsden to Trubel. 'You don't believe we'd vote the way we believe, but the fact is we *would* be voting the way we believe. And that scares you. Doesn't it, Mr Trubel?'

Trubel shook his head slowly, his eyes frigid on Amsden. 'No,' he said. 'That don't scare me, Professor.'

'Look at it this way,' Amsden rushed on.

The Negro burst in, 'You look at it *this* way, charley: you're in contempt of—'

'Let him talk,' Trubel said, waving the Negro's interruption away. He stared at Amsden.

Amsden nodded. 'Let's say we don't vote, the three of us, and you don't vote. That leaves a jury of four. It's not a balanced jury. Let's say your jury of four is split: three of them vote, one each for each one of us three original suspects, and that leaves one vote. So the last vote goes against me or Koster or the Congressman. The final vote would be two to one to one. That means a vote of only half the jury would hang a man. How is that justice?'

Trubel considered it, sighing and sneering and wheezing, and finally he peered up at Lancelot Everybody. 'He makes sense. Maybe I should vote, after all.'

'That's not a good answer,' Amsden said. 'That's the gangster in you talking. Let one suspect vote, but not all three. What's that—Sicilian democracy?'

'He's a gangster,' said Wade, eyes sharp on Trubel. 'Stop expecting democracy.'

'Listen,' scowled Trubel and he rubbed his nose slowly and thoughtfully. 'So if they vote that way—they have to vote *again*.'

'Oh fine,' said Amsden, mockingly. 'And so the second vote would allow a gang-up on whoever had the two votes against him in the first vote.'

Trubel grasped his cane with both hands and slowly hunched forward in his chair, leaning on the cane.

'Mr Trubel wants to say,' began the Negro, 'that in

146

fixing guilt here, the rules are the rules of this seceded republic called Tommy's room, and if you charleys expect like everything's going to be normal and—'

'Shut up, Lanny,' frowned Trubel, still leaning his chin on his hands. He went on meditating.

Amsden was impatient: 'If one of us is really going to be killed, you should at least—'

'Shut up, Professor!' snapped the Negro. 'Mr Trubel is thinking.'

In another minute Trubel slowly sat back. 'Hey, Lanny,' he said. 'Get some cards. And pencils.'

'How many?' asked the Negro.

'Eight,' said Trubel, looking at Amsden. 'Eight cards. Eight pencils.'

'No!' cried Noreen.

'No do!' pleaded the Chinese. 'Listen, Louie—please don't!'

'You going to solve a death in the family with two deaths in the family?' Rexie My Riddle asked Trubel quietly, his unnatural but resolute grin wavering and threatening to vanish for the first time through the night.

'I won't let you do that, Louie,' whined Noreen, taking his head with her hands, forcing him to look up at her. 'All this time you studied, all this time you believed, knowing you were right. Now you think maybe *you* did it. Only, if you did it, *we* did it. I won't let you say that!'

'Let me do right, Noreen,' grunted Trubel, and pulled his large head free, staring down on his cane. 'Lanny.'

'But shit, it isn't even your fault,' moaned Noreen.

'So don't write my name down,' wheezed Trubel. He thinned his eye on the Negro and said more sharply, 'Lanny.'

The Negro walked slowly to the door. The Chinese quietly opened it for him and Lancelot Everybody left the room.

Trubel glanced off into the tension that stilled the room

and presently broke into it to say to Amsden, 'It's no different this way, Professor. If you three try to hang me, and even if I vote against myself—'

'Don't talk like that, Louie!' insisted Noreen.

He frowned at her, then went on to Amsden. '—even if I vote against myself, what have you got? Four votes. If all the other votes go against one of you, what have you got? A deadlock. If the other votes got divided, three votes against me would come out on top. Then I'd be the one—even if I didn't vote against myself. Only, Professor—I'll put up with it. Sometimes you got to take order where you can find it.'

'Louie,' moaned Noreen.

He frowned at her. 'Let me think. I don't want to have doubts, so let me think, Noreen.'

'In a case like that,' said Amsden, 'the only right thing to do would be to call the jury deadlocked and consider everyone acquitted and no one condemned.'

'No,' Trubel turned his large head back and forth, 'no, Professor. No. I went at this too long. I been through it all. No—whoever has the most votes against him, he's guilty. I got to solve this for myself—see?'

'Louie,' Noreen went on begging, 'don't—shit, you blamed yourself enough, all the year. Don't do this, too!'

'If he blamed himself, why are *we* here?' demanded Koster.

Carson City Go, who had during Trubel's self-accusation lost his smile, also lost his American-Chinese diction as he shot back at Koster: 'Because Mr Trubel took his time— *that's* why,' and he added with a sneer, 'important man.' In a moment, though Noreen had been about to speak, he rushed on, 'Because after he investigated things, after he studied, maybe Mr Trubel saw how it was tough to say who was guiltiest, but there wasn't no reason to think one of you creeps didn't make the biggest mistakes in the death of Tommy Lincoln. That's why—important man.'

'I mean shit,' Noreen was insisting to Trubel, 'defendants can't be the jury, Louie. Gee, since when are defendants on the jury?'

'Maybe,' said Wade, 'since Louie Trubel made himself a judge.'

Lancelot Everybody was at the door, being admitted by the Chinese, who had got just about a quarter of his silly bright smile back to greet the Negro.

The room fell silent again, as the Negro slowly passed out cards and pencils, his slow tread bespeaking his unwillingness and his grudging fingers, as he handed cards to the suspects, bespeaking his distrust.

Trubel fingered his pencil nervously, in his fist, rubbing it against his palm, tapping it on the arm of his chair as if he thought it a wee version of his cane. No one wrote, all watching Trubel—as though it were to be a race and Trubel would fire a signal gun.

'Okay,' Trubel said eventually. 'You write one name on your card. You write clear,' he frowned up at Noreen. Then he looked at his own card, as blankly as it looked back at him. 'Then,' he said, 'you turn your card over and put it on the table, there. Then we'll read the cards. One at a time. And they can be inspected. Am I being fair, Professor?'

Amsden nodded sharply with his intense inner excitement.

'Sure,' said Trubel. A slow, thick grin spread out across his long mouth—it was the first real grin that had appeared on his sallow old face through the proceedings and the first indication of any amusement on his part since his strange explosion of laughter. 'Carson City,' he said, 'I don't hear you. When did you ever pass up the chance for side bets? Carson City?'

Carson City Go gazed only remorsefully at his boss.

Congressman Wade sat poised, ready to write—he looked

more than any of them the runner at the starting line, ready to spring.

Trubel scowled around at everyone. 'Write,' he mumbled. He looked up at Noreen. 'Write.'

Wade, who had looked as if he would write instantly, nearly did—but then waited, his mouth just the tiniest bit pursed and open, gazing worriedly at his pencil. When he wrote, he wrote slowly.

Trubel kept nodding at his card, as if it were communicating with him, or as if he could see the writing on the card still before he had put it there. He poised his pencil carefully, shielding the card in his hand, then shook his head and sat back and closed his eyes.

Noreen looked deeply perplexed and even fearful, watching the remote Trubel, as if for a guidance of inspiration. She bit at her pencil and finally, her pencil mincing, dragged a word out across the card.

Behind Wade, Rexie My Riddle balanced his card on the back of the high wing chair and, oddly, wore a tortured expression that did not exclude his accustomed grin, but merely misshaped it. He wiped at his eyes a few times, clacked his tongue and licked at his lips. At last he wrote, his pencil looking uncertain in its manipulation.

Amsden, who had sat still, staring at Trubel, suddenly gave his head a little shake and made a small grunting sound. He set the card on the book he held in his lap and, guarding it with one hand, he wrote quickly. Then he turned the card over and stared gloomily at its blank side.

Carson City Go, by the door, was undergoing a terrible series of facial contortions, snapping his tongue, twisting his neck around, scratching, leering bitterly from Wade to Amsden to Koster, looking pathetically at his own colleagues, licking his teeth and chewing his pencil, squeezing his eyes shut angrily. It was some while before he turned around, set the card against the door and wrote a name down.

Lancelot Everybody, who had moved to the projector

table, stared at Louie Trubel, and Trubel—when he finally opened his eyes—stared at the Negro. The Negro was frowning quizzically, as if still wondering of Trubel what had been the good in adopting this method, or as if Trubel might yet change his mind and readopt his original conception of a restricted jury's duty : discussion and decision with no fourth suspect. The Negro suddenly growled just audibly, bent over the table and wrote a name down. Then, face down, he moved to the table before the sofa and set his card down on it. He faced Trubel glumly.

Trubel muttered something to himself, moved his lips about in consternation and snorted. He leaned forward, once again cupping a hand around his card. He let the pencil pause before he wrote—then carefully wrote down a name, turned the card over and sat back. His mouth opened to emit a wheezing sigh and his eyes just flicked up off of Noreen's—her own eyes prodding him for information.

The Negro slowly went around collecting the face-down cards, and he set them all on top of his own card, shuffled them a bit and set them down on the table.

'Lanny,' said Trubel, then, and still again shut his eyes.

The Negro picked up the cards he had just set down and slowly shuffled them some more, watching Trubel expressionlessly.

Trubel's eyes opened. 'Lanny?'

'Yeah,' mumbled the Negro and he cleared his throat and turned over the card just then on top of the thin pile, his eyes seeming a little startled or perhaps only anxious as he read aloud :

'Congressman Wade.'

Wade sucked in his breath and fastened his eyes to his hands in his lap. He was, for the moment, frozen.

The Negro had turned over another card after passing the first one over for Trubel's inspection, who turned it over to Noreen, who was handing it to Wade himself. It took Wade a minute to free his hand from the brief general paralysis that had grasped him, and he took the card vacant-eyed.

The Negro's voice was brittle and bitter : 'Louie Trubel,' he read, and snapped his arm around to hand the card to Trubel.

Noreen made a small sound, like a whine compressed into an exclamation point, as she received the card immediately from Trubel.

The Negro turned the third card over and tightened his lips as he read :

'Louie Trubel.'

He studied the card briefly, emptily, then again passed the card along to Trubel, who started it around the room.

Suddenly Noreen cried, 'This isn't the way we were going to do it !'

'This is the way we are doing it,' muttered Trubel. 'Lanny?'

The Negro sighed and turned over another card :

'Amsden.'

Amsden blinked stiffly and received the card directly from the Negro. He passed the card over to Koster, who sat with his face white, breathing heavily. Koster's hand shook as he took the card from Amsden.

The Negro had turned over the next card and he read aloud :

'Professor Amsden.'

That card, too, was given first to the teacher.

Amsden scarcely looked at the card, only nodding as he gave it over to Koster. He turned over the book in his lap and began paging through it. The little squints his eyes made suggested he was not pretending to read, but only trying to busy his hands.

The Negro had turned over a new card, and his voice snapped out with clear dissatisfaction :

'Louie Trubel !'

He gave the card to Trubel with a scowl. Trubel shook

his head and passed it on to Noreen, who left her mouth open and forgot to pass the card to Wade.

Koster suddenly drank in breath and he made a small sobbing noise, and could not keep a hint of relief from spurting smile-like onto his mouth : he had just understood that no vote could go against him, and he had been acquitted. The Negro was reading :

'Professor Amsden.'

Trubel nodded while Amsden took the card. Amsden's eyes were a little glazed and, as Noreen had forgotten to pass on a card to Wade, so did Amsden now forget to pass the card to Koster.

'You and me, Professor,' said Trubel, 'we ain't popular in here.'

It took Amsden a moment to work a voice out of himself but he finally said, softly and chokily, 'I think the Trubel vote was just used up.'

Trubel sniffed and shut his eyes. 'Lanny?'

The Negro looked at the last card in his hand, closed his mouth, puckered it, and then just murmured, 'Professor Amsden,' and gave the card to Amsden. Amsden failing to reach out for it, he tossed the card into Amsden's lap, then sighed and went to stand by Louie Trubel's chair.

Amsden managed to get out a cigarette but found his hands would not hold his match. 'Would someone light this damn thing for me?' he whispered.

Cassius Koster at once leaned over to strike one of Amsden's matches for him.

'So,' Amsden choked out over smoke and over-tight muscles, 'how much time do I have?'

'Professor,' said Trubel, studying Amsden's pale face as the teacher inhaled heavily of the smoke. 'Was it a fair vote?'

Amsden made something like a chuckle. 'Democracy in action,' he said quietly and shakily. He dropped his cigarette—Koster hurrying out a hand to pick it up from the sofa for him. 'Thanks,' muttered Amsden, seeing

153

Koster stare at him now in a kind of astonishment of dread. 'So,' Amsden said again, looking at Trubel, 'how much time do I have?'

Trubel shook his head. He pulled out his large pocket watch. 'We all got schedules. Congressman Wade, he's got a busy schedule tomorrow.'

'Don't mean to intrude,' said Amsden, and coughed on his smoke.

'It's late,' said Trubel, putting his watch away.

Amsden tried to chuckle but produced something in the way of a cackle.

'But,' Koster began, his voice almost as tight and unmanageable as Amsden's so that it took him seconds before he could spit words out, 'you aren't really just . . . I mean, you can't just take him—'

Trubel wrinkled his lips, he looked like he may have given Koster either an angry glint or an ironic wink. He was leaning forward after having put his watch away, ready to be lifted from his chair.

The two acquitted men and the one condemned man stared as, with deferent care, Lancelot Everybody and Rexie My Riddle helped Louie Trubel to his feet. Trubel grunted, twisted his mouth, growled in complaint and sighed ponderously once he was leaning on his cane and supported at either side by his men. He looked dully at Amsden.

'Professor?' he said.

Amsden started.

'We want you to come with us, charley,' the Negro told Amsden tonelessly.

Amsden's brows quivered, his mouth spasmed and he slowly rubbed his cigarette out in the ashtray. As he worked to stand up, he found himself trembling and he had to work harder—but did get himself onto his feet, though all he could do for a time was to stand there wavering.

Congressman Wade inquired softly, 'Well, what . . . that is, what's to become of Mr Koster and myself?'

The Negro turned to him. 'Do what you want.'

Trubel frowned at the Chinese. 'Contempt,' he muttered.

Carson City Go nodded and hurried to Wade even as Wade was saying :

'And Professor Amsden,' his voice weak, spiritless, 'isn't there . . . I mean, all of this is lunatic, it's fantastic . . . Mr Trubel, I have to implore you once again : please do not do this !'

But the Chinese blocked Wade's vision of Trubel, smiling and bowing. 'Charge for contempt of court,' he said. 'Thlee hundled dollar ! Better pay fifty per cent contempt charge for condemned gentleman, seventy-five dollar. Court cost, one thousand dollar. Altogether one thousand, thlee hundled seventy-five dollar. Make cheque to cash, please.' He bowed again.

Wade exclaimed : 'One thousand, three hundred seventy-five dollars ! What are you talking about?'

'Cheque please,' smiled the Chinese, holding a hand out.

Wade fumed, but the fuming seethed impositively, stayed inside of him. Confusion, depression and humiliation kept his temper unclear and he drew out his cheque book and quickly wrote off a cheque, tore it free, just managing a humdrum snort as he put it in the hand of Carson City Go. The Chinese bowed and moved over to Koster at the sofa.

'Contempt of court charge, fifty—'

'Just tell me how much !' Koster rasped midway between fury and fright, his voice nearer to horror than indignation. He already had his cheque book out.

'One thousand, two hundled twenty-five dollar,' said Carson City Go. 'Make to cash please.'

Koster dashed out the cheque, just seemed to have the needed strength to tear it from his book, then thought to inspect his wallet and be sure his money was there. He slowly put his wallet and cheque book back into the inner pocket of his coat.

'I don't have to pay?' Amsden joked lightly to the Chinese, who was now beside him.

'Yes,' smiled the Chinese. 'Court cost only. Thlee hundled dollar. Make to cash please.' He held his hand out.

Amsden could not restrain a pale chuckle, but he made no move to write the cheque.

'I'll pay for him!' Koster called out in his raspish voice, and he got himself to his feet.

Amsden blinked at Koster and only chuckled again.

'Carson City's only joking,' said Lancelot Everybody. 'Professor Amsden don't have any money debt. Maybe Mr Trubel wouldn't want the Professor's last cheque going through any of his accounts just after his suicide.'

'Suicide,' whispered Koster, who had brought himself over to stand by Amsden. He gazed with terror into Amsden's eyes, but the teacher's eyes were dazed, so that the sharp terror did not pierce a way into Amsden's intelligence.

'Amsden,' Koster murmured.

Amsden required just a vestigial smile of himself and put his hand out to Koster. When he felt Koster's hand in his, he suddenly squeezed it harder than Koster could have expected : as if Amsden abruptly recognized that Cassius Koster was the last tie Harry Amsden might have with the world he understood, and he was saying goodbye through Koster's unlikely agency to everyone he knew. Then Amsden hid his face from Koster and, with the prodding of the Chinese, stumbled over to Trubel's side. He mumbled in the lightest mumble he could muster, by no means lighthearted, 'Wish I knew what you had against me, Mr Trubel, that made you so sure *I* wouldn't talk if you acquitted me—which, by the way, I wouldn't.'

Trubel faced Amsden empty-faced. 'Professor,' he said. 'I'm a gangster. A professional gambler. An old professional, Professor. You got to be smart. You see?'

Amsden shook his head, staring at the floor.

'I don't gamble,' said Trubel. 'Say—I knew the odds

were heavy against you before we ever got under way here. I knew my boys. I knew the record. Professor, you had bad odds.'

Amsden shut his eyes and nodded. 'I never had a chance. If I got acquitted, you wouldn't have let me go.'

Trubel was being turned and guided by the Negro and Rexie My Riddle, Noreen going ahead to the door. Trubel gazed off at the door as he said, 'No—I'd have let you go. Only I could have told you : I nearly never lose. I don't lose, Professor.'

Amsden glanced only briefly with sickly dilated eyes back at Koster; and the publisher—himself too dizzy to stand—had dropped back to sit at the sofa again, gaping at Amsden helplessly.

'Amsden,' wheezed Trubel. 'You made me doubt myself. I don't like that. In a thing like where my son's life is concerned, I don't want to end my life doubting myself. So I thought I could really lose, when I wrote my own name down. Yeah.'

The door was opened and Trubel looked back at Koster and Wade, then at Amsden :

'Hey—I wonder which one of them voted you down, Amsden. You were right,' Trubel let half of his mouth smirk and watched the bewildered teacher. 'You said you guys would vote the way you believed. You were right. So my luck held.'

Trubel turned away without saying another word to Wade or Koster and shuffled out slowly, between Rexie My Riddle and Lancelot Everybody. The Chinese, behind Amsden, gave the teacher a small push to keep him moving out the door, and Amsden had time for only a hasty and questioning look back at Wade and Koster. Then the Chinese turned, standing alone in the doorway, bowing to the two men who still sat, stupefied, in the room.

'Door stay unlocked now,' Carson City Go smiled. 'Make self home ! You like, you go—any time. Many happy leturn on happy acquittal. You like wait, later we dlive you to bus. You like walk, bus stop number four road one mile to left.' He bowed once more, grinned and pointed a finger at Koster. 'Bang bang!' he said.

The Chinese shut the door.

Koster and Wade sat stiffly, not looking at one another.

Koster kept staring at the floor, his hands mechanically certifying that his shirt was buttoned, straightening his tie. Then he let his hands rest in his lip. Wade kept turning his head this way and that, to look at a wall, the cupboard of books, the window, a chair, the book Amsden had left upon the sofa, the projector, at anything except Koster. Both men breathed heavily, their mouths open.

They both started and turned to the window when they heard the slow muted sea-wave of automobile tyres rolling over gravel. The sound vanished and still neither man looked at the other.

Wade, after some minutes, adjusted his own necktie and blinked momentarily at Koster—then dropped his eyes. 'Well,' he muttered, to himself or to no one. He took out his handkerchief, ran it across his brow, then blew his nose and put the handkerchief away.

Koster was slowly heaving himself to his feet. He did not look at Wade as he plodded unevenly across the room, to the door. Pulling the door open wearily and distrustfully, so that it seemed a heavier door than it was, he stood listening or perhaps wondering if he should say any parting words to the congressman. At length, he turned his head about and glanced curiously at Wade. Then, head down again, he faced the dim corridor and soon—not troubling to close the door—he quietly left the room, his footsteps silent in the corridor.

Wade sat staring at the open door. He was still—measuring his very breathing, it seemed; and he shut his eyes for a time. It was several minutes before he took in his breath deeply, stood up, fixed his tie all over again, cleared his throat and then moved to the door. He stepped into the corridor, looked back into the room and then slowly, soundlessly, as if he were leaving a hospital room, he shut the door.

*

My heavy Carracci-hand rubs up a dubious ink,
Becomes a dubious hand beneath a dubious eye
Upon Sam Johnson's 'petty fort': points of mere order.
Never mind! My fall cannot be great, and I'm compelled:
My brush attacks!—too loud, my calligraphy,
This Eastern moral scrawl in Western script;
But I scribble on, maddened to petty war,
For sweet lacunae of Zen are captured for an armory
For weapons of my foes, those soldier artists
Who—in what? hatred of the West?—misuse the East,
Cheerfully depleting Art's storehouse (Truth)
Only to achieve their ends which are their ends.
They have sacked the *mandala* of its privilege,
Leaving behind its purpose and its principle.
They have mass-produced *samsara* in a needle,
And left disdainfully behind its discipline
In which is all its truth and its reward.
True Zennists are, of Eastern puritans,
The most purely puritanical of all—

More so even than the Chinese, whose neo-puritanism
Is not Oriental Marx but ancient sage and custom.
Mao and Nepal's King know more of Buddha's path
Than, say, Ginsberg, Leary, Beatles or Wanderers.
The potter knows: the crack of stress upon the vessel
Cannot exist except the *vessel* is cherished.
And only in its *being* a crack is Zen aleatory.
Or: in its being undefined Shinto is moral
And remains so—straight until it is defined.
The Eastern modes, so rich in subtle paradox,
Liberate only those who discover Right Limits;
And thus, those modes are boundaries: fences—
Without which the East had not had demarcations
For its inner freedom. Now, it's not possible
 That this bold Carracci-hand should deftly paint
A petty Eastern fort and make it look like Western Man
(Much less Woman—my own, and Tao's apologies!)
Yet I try, with sincerity, to wield the brush
With freedom born of minding freedom's limits:
And seek no image of self-serving liberation,
But only the Dragon's Eye in which men live;
And choose a paradox as subject: 'moral gangsterism':
One view of Eastern thought in Western guise.
This poor scroll I give to my Japanese 'little brother',
My former student now teaching students of his own,
And dedicate it fondly to him:

Nobuo Kuratomi